Appearances
A novel

K. RESHAY

Thanks for the love & support! K. Reshay

ISBN: 1545192820
ISBN 13: 9781545192825

PROLOGUE

Summertime, and the livin' is easy. Fish are jumpin' and the cotton is high. Oh, your daddy's rich and your ma is good-lookin'. So hush, little baby; don't you cry. One of these mornings you're gonna rise up singing. And you'll spread your wings and you'll take to the sky. But till that morning, there ain't nothin' can harm you with daddy and mammy standin' by.

-"Summertime," Billie Holiday

As the radio station played the soothing sounds of Billie Holiday's rendition of "Summertime," Maya's parents navigated the one-way streets, trying to find her dorm on the University of Alabama Campus. It definitely was summertime in the city of Birmingham, Alabama. The sun was shining, and the temperature was ninety-five degrees. The humidity was so thick that two or more showers a day were the norm.

"Dad, there it is—right there!" Maya exclaimed. She was so excited about the new phase in her life. All summer, she'd planned for this day. It was bittersweet, though.

"All right, I want you to know that your mom and I are so proud of you. I know that you'll be successful. I just pray I'm around to see you graduate," Maya's dad said as he pulled into a parking space in front of her new dorm.

"Russell, don't go bringing Maya down, now. She has enough on her plate," Maya's mom said, looking visibly upset at the last comment her husband had made.

"It's okay, Mom. He's not bringing me down, because I know that he'll be here to see me graduate, get married, and have kids." Maya said.

"Well, getting married and having kids should be the last thing on your mind, young lady. In fact, don't forget the little gifts I packed in your yellow bag. Hell, I've been young before," her mother smirked as her dad pretended not to hear.

Maya stepped out of the truck and took a deep breath. The scenery was a bit different from the Memphis city where she lived. She was beginning to get nervous. Sweat beads started to form as she grabbed her things. This would be the first time she'd be away from her dad since he had been diagnosed with colon cancer. She had known this day was coming but had begun to resent it. She wanted to be there for him when he began chemotherapy next month, but he'd told her that taking a year off from school was simply out of the question.

It wasn't until she saw the cute guy walking toward her that Maya began to forget her concern about her dad. It looked like she'd caught the guy's eye as well. He damn near bumped into her dad while he was walking. She laughed, but her dad did not. He knew exactly what the guy was thinking. He just hoped that the values he had instilled in his daughter would prevail.

"Let's see. Here it is, Dad—room seventeen fourteen. I hope my roommate hasn't made it yet. I really want the bed by the window." Maya nervously opened the door to find that she was the first to make it there.

While Maya was getting settled into her room, her roommate was downstairs with her mom. Toni did not want her mom to help her. She wanted to be a grown-up and unpack alone.

"Toni, call me as soon as you get settled. I'm headed to the airport to get your stepfather, then we'll be back. I've been dying to try this restaurant at the Summit called California Pizza Kitchen. I heard it was awesome," Toni's mom said.

"Okay, bye, Mom! See you all shortly." Toni smiled and grabbed her luggage. It was a forced smile. She still was upset with her mom for taking her stepfather back. She knew her mom could do better, but as the saying went, you can't tell a woman in love anything.

As she walked up the stairs, Toni could hear all the conversations around her. Girls were laughing and talking about where they were from. She started to get excited as she searched for her room. The white wall near the middle of the hall was covered with all kinds of fliers. One said that there was a mandatory dorm meeting. Another one in all red said that there was a party that night at the frat house down the street. Toni made a mental note to ask her roommate if she'd like to attend. She couldn't think of a better way to kick off their first night on the college campus. Plus, it would give her a reason to wear the cutoff shorts and backless top she'd bought at Forever 21 earlier that day.

The room door was open, so Toni adjusted her shirt and walked in to find Maya and her parents. "Good afternoon. I'm Toni. It's so nice to meet you," Toni said as she walked over to hug Maya. Maya's parents greeted her and continued unpacking.

"It's nice to finally meet you. I hope you don't mind me getting the bed by the window," Maya said as she noticed her new roommate's beauty.

"Oh, no! Not at all. I'm just glad to be here. It took forever for them to find me a dorm," laughed Toni.

Maya's mom was busy hanging curtains. Toni noticed that she was not being as polite as Maya's dad was. She looked worried.

"Well, looks like we are all done here. Toni, we were going to get some lunch. Would you like to come with?" Maya's mom asked.

"Oh, I'd love to, but my mom and stepdad will be back in about an hour, and we're going to eat. Thanks for inviting me, though. It was really nice meeting you all," she said as she shook their hands. "Maya, before I forget, there's a party later tonight at the Kappa House. Let's go?" she whispered.

"I'm down," said Maya as she winked and walked out the door.

Toni smiled as she looked around her new home away from home. The walls were white. On Maya's side were pictures of her and her family. Her bed was made up with a dark-pink comforter set. Her clothes were still packed up, but from the curtains and comforter set, it wasn't hard to guess what her favorite color was.

Toni turned on her radio and began to unpack. The soothing sounds of Aaliyah's "4 Page Letter" filled the room. Toni hummed the vocals as she danced around, thinking about the boyfriend she'd left back home in Biloxi, Mississippi. She quickly unpacked and called her mom to tell her she was ready.

Toni's dinner didn't last as long as she thought it would. Her stepfather acted impatient during dinner. He just had to get a shower and settle in before it got too late. *The damn nerve of him,* she thought. Here she was trying to enjoy time with her mom, and he was busy pushing her away. She hugged them good-bye, went back to her dorm room, and began reading *The Bluest Eye*, by Toni Morrison.

Maya also said her good-byes as her parents prepared for the long ride back to Memphis. They had eaten at Olive Garden, one of her favorite restaurants. She tried to hide the sadness she felt. She was so worried about her dad. She'd never lost anyone close to her. But he had assured her at dinner that he would be fine.

Holding back her tears, Maya made her way back to the dorm room. She was definitely a daddy's girl. She couldn't help but think that this would be the last time she would see her father in good spirits. She kept imagining him lying in a hospital bed with tubes in his nose and mouth. She shuddered at the image.

"Hey, Maya! Is everything okay?" Toni asked, looking concerned. Although they had just met, she felt oddly close to her new roommate.

"I'm fine, girl. I just am really close to my dad, and he's sick."

"Oh, I'm sorry to hear that. Is there anything I can do?" Toni was not comfortable enough to ask for details just yet.

"Just keep him in your prayers, if you don't mind. Life is just crazy right now. Anyway, what time is this party?" Maya asked, plopping down on her bed, exhausted from moving, traveling, and emotion.

Toni grabbed the flier. "Let's see; it's at ten. The dorm meeting is at seven."

"Cool. Well, I guess I need to find something to wear. So where are you from?" asked Maya as she went through her closet.

"I'm from Biloxi, Mississippi. Grew up with both of my parents until my dad decided he no longer wanted to be with my mom, or any woman, in fact."

Toni's revelation made Maya flash back to seeing her father kiss his so-called out-of-town cousin.

Toni had walked home from her basketball practice. She was upset because the coach had made her run suicides for missing two lay-ups in a row. She thought she heard what sounded like her dad in their garage. As she approached, she saw her dad hugging, then kissing his cousin. She was puzzled by the whole thing. She knew what she was seeing was very odd, but she was only eleven and was not old enough to really understand. It wasn't until she overheard her parents arguing years later that she understood what she had seen. She never told her mom about it, or anyone, as a matter of fact.

"Damn, I'm sorry to hear that, Toni. I can't imagine what that must feel like," said Maya, walking over to comfort her newfound friend.

"It's okay. I figured out that when it comes to matters of the heart, you can't help who you love. So where are you from?" she asked, not wanting to reveal any more.

"I'm from M-Town, or Memphis, Tennessee. My parents have been married almost twenty-six years. I love seafood, barbecue, and pizza. I love music, especially blues, and I plan to major in business."

Both girls burst out laughing. They felt like they were interviewing for a job. Maya continued to try to put outfits together as they continued their conversation. She hoped to see the guy she'd locked eyes with earlier that day at the party. With that thought in mind, she opted to wear her light-blue BeBe dress. It had cutout sides and fit her slim frame perfectly.

The girls continued to become acquainted right up until it was time for the dorm meeting. They discovered that they had a lot in common. Both girls liked each other and were glad they were roommates.

After the meeting, they showered, dressed, and applied each other's makeup carefully. They figured there was no better time than the present to see what fine men their new campus offered. Toni just wanted to look, though. She loved her man back home.

The frat house was packed. People were standing outside, on the balcony, and near the parking area. The girls had lots of eyes on them as they approached. Once they entered the house, the smell of marijuana mixed with sweat made them look at each other sideways.

Maya frowned at a girl who was dancing. She was showing practically everything her mama gave her. Toni whispered, "I guess her major is ass and titties?" Both girls laughed at the joke.

The DJ decided to slow the mood down. Tyrese's "Sweet Lady" filled the room. Guys were pulling girls close, and the ladies headed toward the kitchen and bar area for a drink. Toni was in front, and Maya was following close behind her.

Maya felt someone pull on her arm. She turned to see that it was the guy from earlier that day. She tapped on Toni's shoulder and told her that she'd be right back. Toni couldn't see the guy, but said okay.

"So, we meet again. I'm Ty. And you are?" he asked.

"I'm Maya. It's nice to officially meet you." She blushed as they began to slow dance.

"It's nice to officially meet you, as well," he said.

They danced and talked during the next few slow songs. When the music started changing, Ty asked Maya if she wanted to talk outside. She told him that she needed to go get her friend but would be back.

She found Toni chilling by the kitchen area. "Hey, are you cool?" she asked.

"Yeah, I'm ready to go, though. My man has called me and is already tripping about me being at a party," said Toni, visibly irritated.

"Okay, that's fine with me. I have an eight o'clock class anyway. Let me tell my friend that we're leaving," Maya said.

The ladies walked outside, and Maya spotted Ty on the patio. "I'll be right back, girl," she said. Toni finally noticed the guy Maya was talking to. *Good pick, girl*, she thought.

"Okay, I gave him my number, so we can go now," Maya laughed. The two ladies walked back to their dorm and began their journey to a new friendship.

Simple enough, right? *Sigh…*

1

MAYA

"Call the caterer, find a photographer, book the chapel and so on and so on! Damn, how in the hell am I going to get all this shit done before noon?" Maya huffed.

With her nuptials approaching fast, Maya was a complete wreck. Having fired her coordinator because she thought she was incompetent, Maya was left to pick up all the pieces. She didn't care, though. All she cared about was becoming Mrs. Sims. Once she was married, she would finally be able to have the life she always wanted. Her best friend Toni was already married, and Maya couldn't wait to add wife to her list of accomplishments, as well.

Maya had dated Toni's husband, Ty, in their freshman and sophomore year of college. She'd thought things were going great for them until she caught him and Toni having sex in the shower of their dorm. As she looked over her balcony, her mind drifted to that day.

It was autumn, and the leaves were beginning to change colors. Maya loved that time of year. She was wearing an amber-colored scarf. She absolutely loved it because it was a gift from Ty. He never bought her much, but the little things mattered to Maya back then.

That morning seemed a little odd, though. The wind wasn't blowing, and it was more chilly than usual. She made hot chocolate before she left and was in a really good mood. She'd checked in with Ty on her way to class and couldn't wait to see him later for lunch.

She remembered scribbling Ty's name on her notebook. She even wrote hers alongside his, as Mrs. Weeks. She longed for the day that she would marry her Prince Charming.

Once she'd made it back from class, she noticed Ty's keys on her dresser, but no Ty. She wondered how he'd gotten into the room, but remembered that Toni had a late class that day. She must have let him in before she left. Maya didn't think much of it. She figured he'd just gone to use the restroom. But when fifteen minutes turned into thirty, Maya began to wonder what in the world he could be doing.

She poked her head out of the door and heard moaning coming from the bathrooms down the hall. Not wanting to draw too much attention to herself, she eased down there to see who it was. As soon as she got closer, she noticed that the moaning sounded familiar. It was definitely Ty. She snatched the door open and followed the moaning straight to the showers. There were Ty and Toni, fucking wildly under cascading water.

She ran over and pushed them into the wall, then grabbed Toni by her hair, and the two started fighting. Ty ran over to break up the fight. During all of the commotion, some of the other girls in the dorm came to see. It was a complete mess.

"Calm down, Maya! Please, I'm sorry!" Ty yelled.

"Don't tell me to calm down, Ty! How could you? And how could you, Toni? I thought you were my friend! How could you sleep with my boyfriend? How could you? You know how much I love Ty!" Maya cried.

"I'm sorry, Maya. I'm sorry. I didn't mean to do this. It just happened. You've got to believe me," Toni lied.

Deep down, Toni knew that she wasn't sorry, but she hadn't planned on being caught in the act, either. She tried to cover up the fact that she was relieved that she could finally be out in the open with how she felt about Ty.

Shortly after, Maya moved out. Toni and Ty came clean and told her they wanted to be together, they just hadn't known how to tell her because she was so in love. Maya was the bigger person. She allowed her relationship to end and watched their relationship begin—out in the open, of course.

Secretly, though, Maya was devastated. She had never been betrayed before. Toni was like a sister to her, and Ty was the love of her life. She suffered from depression for years because of that. She struggled with her self-esteem. She always wondered why she wasn't good enough for Ty. This made her question if she'd ever be good enough for any man.

Despite all of the drama, Maya and Toni had remained friends. Now, ten years later, Ty and Toni were happily married with a beautiful daughter, a daughter to whom Maya was godmother.

A motorist's horn knocked Maya out of her reminiscing session and back to reality. She stepped back inside from the balcony and decided to make herself a mocha latte. It somehow always made her feel better and helped prepare her for the day.

Now, Maya had found a man of her own. She had been introduced to her fiancé Steven through Ricky. Ricky and Ty were best friends. Since they all ran in the same circles, Ricky had thought they would hit it off. This match proved to be a perfect one.

Steven was a great guy. He around six feet tall, slender, and handsome. He was a clean-cut guy with a goatee. His skin was a dark, milky chocolate. He liked long walks in the park and staying up all night talking, and had a great sense of humor. He also was a prominent attorney.

Maya cared deeply for him, but she wasn't in love with him. In fact, the only man she had ever loved was Ty. Ty was not very attractive, but his confidence and personality more than made up for it. He was about five feet ten. He had a muscular build. He always put Maya in mind of the actor Derek Luke. Since Ty was no longer in the picture, so to speak, she felt like this may be her only chance to get married and have a family.

She and Steven settled into a relationship rather quickly. Maya thought that somehow Ty would be jealous that she was with a great guy, a guy his best friend had introduced her to, nonetheless. In Maya's delusional mind, she thought that Ty knew he'd made a mistake in choosing Toni. Every time they were all together, she would look in vain for clues to solidify this notion. But throughout the years, Ty had never given her one sign that he was still interested.

Maya went on appearing to be the perfect best friend. She would always make sure she was as beautiful as she could be whenever the gang would meet up. Maya was around five feet, eight inches tall, and slender. She wore her hair in a short, modern pixie cut. She had a dark complexion and big, dark-brown eyes. She didn't have curves, so she accentuated her body by wearing mostly dresses. She was average by most men's standards.

Physically, she was no comparison to Toni. Toni was beautiful at both ends of the spectrum. She had a caramel-brown complexion and flawless skin. She was what many men would call thick. She was phat in all the right places. Her hair, although long, was always kept neatly in a bun. She was a simple woman who had never had to work. She was a homemaker. Taking care of their daughter and their home was her life. In college, she could have had her pick of whoever she wanted, but she wanted Ty.

Maya was more of a go-getter than Toni. She couldn't stand the notion of being a homemaker. She liked making her own money. She often tried to make Toni jealous by bragging about all of her accomplishments. She tried to prove that she was the better woman every chance she got. It's a wonder that Toni could stand it. Surely, she was hip to what Maya was up to all these years. A woman knows when another woman is jealous of her. Some remove those types of friends from their lives, but Toni didn't.

Maya began selling real estate right out of college. She had recently gained a name for herself by establishing a wealthy clientele who wanted to live in Pemberbrook

Commons. The houses in that neighborhood ranged in the millions. She worked for Regal Real Estate. When her boss found out her fiancé worked for Wilshire and Associates, a prestigious law firm, he quickly placed her in charge of Pemberbrook. Her fiancé's career allowed her to meet wealthy businessmen and colleagues, all of whom wanted to live in Pemberbrook.

"Hi, this is Maya Fisher. We spoke a few weeks ago regarding the chapel rental. Is June seventh still available?" she asked. "Great! I will be by there this afternoon with the payment."

Maya hung up her cell phone and checked the chapel rental off of her list. She then made several calls to photographers. The one she really wanted was booked, so she decided to go with the photographer she'd hired for their engagement photos.

She was glad that she'd taken off for a few weeks. This wedding planning was time consuming, and with Steven out of town on business, she didn't have any help. She could have asked Toni, but decided against it. Maya wanted her matron of honor to be shocked when she saw Maya's wedding. No way was she going to spoil the surprise.

Since Toni and Ty had gotten married at the courthouse, Maya was determined to show her friend what a dream wedding looked like. She was going to make sure her wedding had all the trimmings. There would not be a stone left unturned. This had to be the wedding of the summer.

After finishing up her mocha latte, Maya grabbed her purse and began to look around her gorgeous condo. She had made it a point to have the best condo on the block. It was at the top of her building. The wide windows made the white-and-gold rooms look breathtaking. The views were exceptional. From her balcony, Maya could see the beautiful city of Birmingham. Although she would miss it, it didn't compare to the luxurious home that awaited her and Steven in Pemberbrook. Birmingham, Alabama, was definitely her city, and she was ready to take it over.

Their new home sent the ultimate message of prestige. It was on a gorgeous three-acre lot nestled in the beautiful community of Mountain Brook. It came equipped with five bedrooms, an extralarge master suite, and a beautiful pool. All Maya thought of when picking it out was the look on Toni and Ty's faces when they entered her home for the first time. Their mouths would drop in awe of her beautiful home. She wanted Ty to resent Toni for that.

Toni and Ty lived modestly. They had a nice three-bedroom, two-bath home in the suburbs of Vestavia Hills. There was no comparison to Pemberbrook, of course, but it had a nice, cozy feeling when you entered. Toni had taken the time to decorate it herself, unlike Maya, who had hired Pierre Gordon, a well-known decorator. Maya would turn up her nose when she entered, as if she was royalty. She acted like Toni and Ty were mere peasants to her. She would often laugh to herself at how Ty had settled for such a meager life with Toni.

With friends like Maya, who needed enemies?

2

TONI

Toni was finishing up the last load of laundry when her phone beeped. She knew the familiar sound. It was Maya's beep. She rolled her eyes as she ignored the text and completed the task at hand. After she put away the clothes, she walked over to the counter and looked at her message. "Hi, your dress is ready. Please stop by to get it today," she read aloud.

Wow, she thought. She would be glad when this wedding was over. Maya was driving her crazy with all of the texts. But she was happy for her friend. She knew that Steven was a great guy and would help provide the life Maya deserved. She knew Maya wanted a family, so Steven was right on time with his proposal.

Toni had helped pick out the ring and planned the whole engagement event. Steven had called her and said that he wanted to propose, but had no idea what to do.

He said he knew that she was Maya's best friend and knew more about her than anyone. Toni had been ecstatic.

Steven had met Toni at Maya's favorite jewelry store, Diamonds Direct. Toni had known exactly which ring to pick. It was like hers, but hers was only one carat. She knew Maya liked her ring, but she wouldn't dare get the same one. Toni had opted for one that was two carats bigger than hers. Although the price had been a few thousand more than what Steven wanted to spend, he had obliged.

Toni also knew that Maya loved Robins, a quaint, up-scale restaurant in downtown Birmingham. Maya would often go there to get her favorite dish, chicken and spin-ach fettuccine. Toni had asked Maya to meet her there for dinner.

Once they'd walked in, Steven had gotten on one knee and presented Maya with a gorgeous, three-carat, princess-cut diamond ring. People had gasped at the sight of it. Toni had smiled from ear to ear. She'd done a good job.

The whole gang had been there—everyone except Ricky. Toni couldn't believe the lame excuse he'd given as to why he couldn't attend. She'd thought that of all people, Ricky would be there. He was the one who had hooked Maya and Steven up, for goodness' sake!

Maya had no idea how big a part her friend had played in her engagement. But rather than being filled with joy, Maya had been too busy shoving her ring in Toni's face, comparing it to hers.

"Girl, look at the size of this rock. Steven has definitely outdone himself this time. Tell Ty he is going to have to step up his game," she'd bragged.

Toni hoped that once Maya got married and started a family of her own, it would put an end to the unspoken rivalry she had with Toni. Toni wasn't naïve. She knew that Maya took digs at her every chance she got. She had grown to take blow after blow. After all these years, she knew her best friend still loved and wanted her husband. She never told Ty, though. Ty may have picked up on it, but he never said anything to her about it.

Toni laughed to herself. She knew she was wrong for what she had done to Maya, but she had been young. Her mind went back to their college days as she washed the dishes.

She remembered liking Ty the moment Maya introduced them. He was a handsome man. He was an engineering major and seemed to have his head on straight. She was happy for her friend. But soon, she started to notice that Ty would come around when he knew that Maya wasn't there. She brushed it off at first, but Ty began coming on to her. Her first instinct was to tell her friend what kind of creep she was dating, but she was so attracted to him that she started liking the attention. Toni knew that Maya loved Ty, but convinced herself it was just harmless flirting.

It wasn't until Ty showed up one morning after Maya went to class that Toni could no longer hold back. Maya used to tell her how good Ty was in bed. She said that his dick talked to her. She said he was the only man to make her cum over and over. Toni would take in every detail. She listened as Maya told her what her man's turn-ons were. He loved to do it standing up, she would say. She said his dick was big and long enough to stroke her in every position. She said he enjoyed giving and getting head. Maya bragged about him so much that Toni wanted to see for herself.

She'd actually gotten a little glimpse of what he had to offer when she walked in on them one time. Ty had Maya pinned up against the wall, and they both were naked. Toni quickly ran out of the room, but not before seeing what looked like a nine- or ten-inch dick bobbing back and forth as they scrambled for clothes. She thought she'd noticed a slight smirk on Ty's face, as if he wanted her to see what she was missing.

A few weeks after that, Ty knocked on the door as Toni was getting ready to go shower—or at least, that was the plan. Little did he know, she had already showered and was masturbating when he knocked. She wanted to make sure she had enough sexual energy to complete her act of seduction. Masturbating to the memory of Maya's voice describing how good Ty's dick was along with its image made the anticipation unbearable. He was right on time, too. Toni was just about to climax. She licked her lips and smiled.

She knew that on Tuesdays, he would stop by before his class, knowing that Maya was gone to hers. She seductively opened the door. Ty's eyes nearly popped out of his head. Toni had on a pink silk robe and had a towel wrapped around her head. Her pussy was throbbing so hard, she was sure he could hear it. Toni loved Maya like a sister, but she had to see what type of sex this man possessed. There had been months of sexual tension between them, and she had to obey the laws of attraction.

She pulled him into the room and started kissing him. He wanted it, too. He had wanted Toni the first day he was introduced to her.

Toni grabbed his hand and led it to her moistness. His manhood instantly became aroused. He stuck two fingers inside of her, then pulled them out and savored each drop in his mouth. She tasted good, way better than Maya.

Toni knew she had him. She grabbed his dick, and it was in full salute. She dropped to her knees and pulled it out. There it was, ten inches in all of its thickness and glory. Women see the light when they run up on a big, juicy dick. It's like the angels opening up the gates of heaven, singing alleluia. She began licking it around the top, just like Maya had told her she did. She did it just like Maya had said he liked it.

Toni started sucking slowly. She wanted to make sure to savor every bit of him. He liked it. His eyes rolled into the back of his head. She bobbed her head from side to side, taking him in her wet mouth. She could feel him about to cum. She went faster until he came down her throat. It was ecstasy. She licked every drop from around his dick. Ty moaned loudly.

Toni stood up, proud of her accomplishment. She pushed Ty back on the bed and slowly moved her pussy to his face. He licked his lips in anticipation of what he had already savored. She started moving slowly back and forth on his face. His tongue was doing swirls in and out. It felt so good. His tongue was long and thick. She could feel every inch of it. The more she moved, the faster he licked. Toni could no longer hold it. She came all over his face. He lapped up every drop of her. She moaned loudly as he continued slurping up all of her sweetness.

She wasn't about to let him go. She got up, pulled up his pants and led him to the bathroom. She knew that Maya came back to the dorm room after her class, but she refused to let him leave without feeling every inch of him inside her.

Toni led him to the bathroom and looked around to make sure no one was in there. She turned on the shower and dropped her robe. Ty's mouth hung open. This woman was beautiful to him. He took in every inch of her body as he undressed. The passion between the two was undeniable. They started kissing and panting heavily, as if they couldn't connect fast enough. He sucked and licked her breasts and neck. Toni couldn't stand it anymore. She lifted up one leg and guided him inside of her. He filled every crevice. She came instantly. Then he lifted up her other leg and began stroking her very fast. She knew he loved to do it standing up, and he was great at it. His dick felt so good that she secretly thanked her friend for introducing them. He went in and out so hard that Toni began to lose all thoughts of being caught. She finally knew what Janet Jackson meant in the song "Anytime, Anyplace." She just knew she wanted him and that it felt good. And there was no way she was going to give him back to Maya.

She had to admit, though, being caught was one of the most embarrassing moments of her life. She never thought that Maya would actually catch them in the act, let alone attack her. Then all of the other girls came in and saw them. They started calling her a whore and slut in the weeks that followed.

It wasn't until Maya moved out that the remorse came. Toni remembered the look on her friend's face as she packed up her belongings. They hadn't spoken in weeks, and now Maya was moving out. Toni figured it would all blow over and they would work things out. When Maya no longer returned her calls, she knew she had to sit down with her friend to make things right.

She called Maya and invited her and Ty to Railroad Park. She thought it was a neutral enough place to air things out. And if Maya happened to run up on her like she had in the shower, they'd have *plenty of space. Ty wouldn't be able to help his ex then. Come to think of it, he had run to Maya before defending Toni. She made a mental note to speak to him about that later.*

Toni was the first to arrive. She found a spot and texted the others to let them know where she was. Ty arrived next. He was dressed in his usual gray sweats and a white T-shirt. Toni wished he hadn't worn those pants. That print made her want to skip the kumbaya shit and get down to business between the sheets.

Maya arrived twenty minutes late. She walked up with her head high, wearing a black hat that covered her face a bit.

"Hey Maya. How are you?" Toni asked.

"I'm well, and you? How about you, Ty?" Maya asked, not really giving a damn how they were. Ty nodded instead of speaking. His head was hanging low. He was still remorseful.

"Maya, I asked you to meet us here today because we need to clear the air. I miss you, and I'm so sorry about the way things turned out. Believe mem we didn't plan for this to happen. It's kind of complicated, you see," Toni explained.

"What she means is, we wanted to tell you. We just couldn't find the words," Ty explained.

"Couldn't find the words? Are you kidding me? How about 'Maya, I do not want to be with you. I want your best friend.' See, that wasn't so hard." Tears formed in Maya's eyes as she spoke. "Ty, I trusted you. I trusted you with my life. Did you think of me? Did you once think of me and my love for you? Or were you too busy thinking about screwing this skank?" she yelled.

"Wait a minute Maya! I'm not a skank. Maybe if you knew how to please your man, he wouldn't be looking elsewhere," Toni stated bluntly.

"Elsewhere? Elsewhere is where he should have been looking if that were the case, Toni. Not right under my nose. Not with my best friend. You should have said no. As my friend, you should have said no out of respect for me. There are hundreds of men on that campus. Why mine, Toni? Why?" Maya asked with tears falling down her cheeks and her eyes planted on Ty. Her light pink shirt was decorated with teardrops now.

"Why? Maybe you pushed me to it, Maya. Ever thought about that? When Damon broke up with me, you acted like you didn't even care. You were so busy bragging on Ty. Maybe if you would have kept your mouth shut about how good he was in bed, I might not have even thought about it," Toni snapped back.

"Bitch, take some responsibility for your shit! When Damon broke up with you, it was my shoulder you cried on for weeks. It was me who used my credit card to rent a car to drive your ass to and from Biloxi to see him all the time, since his sorry ass would never come see you. And the fucking thanks I get is you taking my man while I made sure you saw yours?" Maya yelled as Ty calmly walked away. He wanted to speak to Maya alone. He knew how hurt she was. He felt horrible.

"I'm taking responsibility. That's why I'm here. I'm sorry, Maya. I wish it hadn't happened, but I'm glad it did. I love Ty. I love him, and we are going to be together. But I want you to be okay with it, and I want my friend back. Let's not let a guy come between us," Toni said.

"Fine! I accept your apology. I'm okay with it. Is that what you want to hear?" Maya asked.

"Know that I love you Maya. I want us to be friends again. I miss you," Toni pleaded.

"Okay, we'll talk later. I'm sure you want to catch up with Ty down there. I'll be fine. I wish you all the best," Maya said. She walked away without looking back.

Toni knew that Maya never truly forgave her after their conversation. She wanted her friend to understand that she was sorry, but she secretly wanted the go ahead to be out in the open with her relationship with Ty. She wasn't about to let him go.

Many times, Toni felt guilty. She out of all people knew how much her friend loved Ty, but *all is fair in love and war,* she thought.

As she heard the dryer's timer go off, Toni came back to the present. *One more load and then I'll be done,* she thought. She smiled as she grabbed her keys and headed out the door to pick up her dress.

3

TY

"Ricky, you have not been answering my calls or texts all week, man. The tuxedo fitting is tomorrow. Call me back," Ty said to Ricky's voice mail. His best friend had been avoiding him, and he didn't know why. It wasn't like Ricky to not answer a call or text from him. So Ty decided to pay him a visit to get to the bottom of it.

Ty and Ricky had been friends for so long that they were like brothers. They told each other everything and were always there for one another. But ever since Ricky's wife Laila had suddenly divorced him a few months ago, Ricky had been withdrawn.

Ricky lived about two hours from Birmingham in Douglasville, Georgia. Ty took off early to check on his friend in hopes of making it back in time for dinner. As he glided onto the interstate, Ty thought about the upcoming weekend. He couldn't believe that he was going to be a groomsman in the wedding of his ex-girlfriend. After all of these years, he still considered Maya an ex. He hated that she and Toni continued to be friends. He knew by the way she looked at him that there was still something there on her end, but he never mentioned it to Toni. The last thing he wanted was for his wife to be jealous of the woman she'd stolen him from.

He was glad that Maya was finally getting married. Back in school, she would tell him how she couldn't wait to get married and have kids. She was a nice girl back then, but deep down, he knew that she had never forgiven him for choosing Toni.

Maya was a decent girl. Any man would be glad to have her on his arm, but Toni was something special to him. No woman had ever commanded his attention like Toni. All he could think about after meeting her was making her his woman. He would fantasize about Toni when he slept with Maya. He didn't want to destroy their friendship, so he had to test what type of friend Toni was. He wanted to know if she was the type of friend to tell or the type of friend to keep quiet. He found his answer soon enough.

He was actually relieved when Maya caught them. If she hadn't, he didn't think he would have had the heart to tell her to her face that he was interested in her best friend. Getting a blow job from his crush was just the welcome mat he needed, though. He remembered wondering how in the hell she knew exactly how he wanted to be fucked. It was as if she knew his every move. He chalked it up to her just being made for him.

Ty thought back to the hurt on Maya's face. It was a look that he never wanted to be responsible for again, and he prayed that no man would ever put a look like that on his daughter's face. He felt awful for what he had done. But Toni somehow convinced him to believe that Maya understood and was cool with the whole situation.

He, on the other hand, was not. While most men wouldn't feel shit about sleeping with women who were friends, Ty couldn't stand it. He constantly felt reminded of what he had done. The guilt was sometimes hard on him. He knew what he had done was wrong.

Oftentimes, he felt that Maya purposely stayed around to see how everything would play out. He would catch her asking Toni very personal questions about their finances and goals, especially when their daughter was born. He always kept quiet, but he never really considered his wife's friend an actual one. He hoped that once this wedding was done, he would begin seeing less and less of Maya.

Once he had taken the exit to Ricky's house, Ty tried calling again. He was never the type to just show up on people unannounced, but this time, he had to make an exception. Still no answer. As he took the left at the stop sign, he slowed down. Steven's blue Corvette was parked in front of Ricky's house.

He wondered what Steven was doing over there this early in the afternoon. From what Toni had told him, he was supposed to be on a business trip this week. He pulled up behind Steven's car and got out. As soon as Ty closed his car door, he could hear yelling. He ran to the door to see what was going on, but something he heard made him stop dead in his tracks.

"I love you, Ricky! I love you! But what do you want me to do? I can't call off my wedding. I'm sorry about your wife, man. I promise you I'm sorry, but what would you have me do? I can't continue to live my life with you behind closed doors. And what about Maya? She doesn't deserve this, either. I love her," cried Steven.

"Steven, are you fucking kidding me? I lost everything because of you. How do you think I'm supposed to feel, watching you marry that superficial bitch?" Ricky yelled.

"She's not a bitch. And you introduced us. Why?" asked Steven.

"I introduced you to her because I thought it was what you wanted. I mean, what Ty wanted. Look, he'd never understand why I wouldn't want to play matchmaker. You said you wanted to leave me alone. But here we go again, sleeping together. Where did you tell her you were this week, huh? She doesn't even bother to call you. She just wants a fucking title, and your crazy ass is going to give it to her!" Ricky screamed.

Ty had to blink over and over. He couldn't believe what he was hearing. He tiptoed toward the window once the yelling stopped. He could see the two men embracing, kissing, and then Ricky picked Steven up and carried him out of sight. Ricky was wearing only a pair of boxers, and Steven was naked.

Ty ran back to his car and sped off. Two blocks down the road, he pulled over and vomited. He was in total shock. For years, he had been friends with this guy. He'd had no idea he was gay. No idea at all. And fucking Steven, no less. In college, Ricky was the man. He had hoes left and right throwing it at him, and he was the type of man who could catch. They loved his chocolate skin and hazel eyes. The curly high-top fade he'd had didn't make it any better, either. *How in the hell could I have missed this memo?* Ty wondered. He didn't know what to think. All he knew was that Steven was marrying his wife's best friend, and the shit was about to hit the fan—and the walls.

4

RICKY

"Damn, you feel good, baby. Um, don't stop. Right there. That's it," Ricky moaned.

He licked his lips as he received head from Steven. It felt so good. Steven's lips and mouth were so wet and inviting. Steven could deep throat his dick effortlessly. The feeling was unreal. He grabbed Steven's head and guided it as it bobbed back and forth on his member. He knew that Steven couldn't wait to taste him again, and he was happy to oblige. Soon, he was about to cum, and Steven eagerly sucked in anticipation. Once he came, he did it all over Steven's face. Steven loved it. He was Ricky's little bitch and proud of it.

While Steven was in the shower, Ricky checked his phone. More missed calls from Ty. He decided to at least text him back. He hated avoiding his friend, but he was dealing with way too much shit. Here he was in love with a man who was about to get married. The sad part about it was that he couldn't even own up to the fact that he was gay. He'd been gay as long as he could remember.

Ricky was absolutely gorgeous. He looked like Morris Chestnut mixed with a little Idris Elba. He'd always been a ladies' man. In college, he was the star of the basketball team.

Growing up in the South, Ricky was inclined to keep his thoughts about being with other men to himself. He'd overheard his parents commenting on the Miller boy, who was beaten to death by a group of teenagers because he was gay. His dad stated that he'd gotten what he deserved. And his mom agreed. Ricky was in total disbelief. He had never heard his parents speak like that before. Since that time, he'd never dared to tell anyone about his feelings.

He played the part of the promiscuous teenage boy very well, oftentimes sleeping with several girls at the same time. It wasn't until he went to college that he explored being with men. But he knew that if his parents ever found out about him, they would never speak to him again.

Ty had no idea about Ricky's inclinations, and he wanted to keep it that way. He and Ty were like brothers. But even brothers keep secrets from one another. He didn't want to risk losing their friendship, even though he knew Ty was not the type of guy to stop being friends with someone just because of his or her sexual preference.

Ricky was snapped back into reality when Steven's cell beeped. He reached over to see a text from Maya. "Hey, baby, I hope everything is going well at the seminar. I know you will be great. I can't wait to become Mrs. Sims. Xoxo," he read aloud.

Ricky tossed the phone on the bed and lay on his back. He'd never thought that Steven would actually go through with this whole marriage facade. He detested Maya. She was a fake bitch. He knew she did all she could to put his friend and his wife down. He would ask Ty how in the hell he continued to allow that tramp around them, and Ty would always lay that whole "Remember when I used to date her in school?" bullshit on him.

He knew that Maya was up to no good, but Steven fell in love. Ricky had only introduced him to Maya to get Ty off of his back. Once Ty had met Steven and found out he was single, he'd stayed on Ricky to hook the two up. Ricky had obliged, knowing that it would only be a matter of time before Steven realized Maya wasn't even worth being his beard. Now, two years later, this idiot was about to make the biggest mistake of his life, and Ricky just couldn't let that happen.

Tears rolled down his face as he recalled the letter his wife had left stating that she'd caught him and Steven together. He'd met Laila during their senior year in college. She was absolutely perfect for him. She was the type of girl a man would be glad to bring home to meet his parents. He knew he was gay, but he thought that being with a woman exclusively would curb his appetite for men.

For a few years, it seemed like it had worked. He still had the urge sometimes, but he never acted on it. But when he met Steven, he could no longer fight the urge. They immediately began sleeping together. During this time, Steven was introduced to Ty.

Ricky and Steven became too comfortable, though. Shit just wasn't adding up for Laila, so she hired a private investigator and found out that they were meeting up on Saturdays at the Hamilton Hotel off of Monroe Avenue. She discreetly got a room key from the hotel attendant. She crept into the hotel room and found the two of them having sex. They were so into it that they didn't even hear her until the door slammed shut. They jumped up and rushed to the door, but only saw what looked like a lady running down the stairs. They thought it may have been someone who'd gotten the wrong key or something.

The following afternoon, Ricky returned home from his so-called coaching camp to an empty house, a folder full of photos, and a letter from Laila on his kitchen counter. He felt his heart drop as he looked at each photo. He began to cry uncontrollably. Not because of the fact that Laila had left him, though. He was crying because he feared she would expose his secret.

He didn't regret that Laila had trusted him and would never look at men the same way again. He didn't regret the fact that he had broken his vows. He didn't even fear that he might have brought his wife a sexually transmitted disease (Steven had said he didn't like condoms). The selfishness of it all was undeniable.

Steven acted like he didn't care when Ricky called him and told him the news. He was more relived than anything. He thought that he and Ricky could finally come out of the closet and really have a great life together. Steven was worried about coming out, but he knew with Ricky beside him, they could conquer the world.

Once Ricky made it clear that coming out was absolutely not an option, Steven's heart broke. He had really grown to love Ricky. He thought about him all the time. He knew he loved Maya too, but it wasn't like the love he had for Ricky. His love for her was more of a tolerable love. His love for Ricky was an unattainable love, but he still wanted it all the same.

Steven knew that Maya was ready to get married and have children. He decided that since he couldn't have the one he loved, he would love the one he was with.

5

MAYA

"Thanks again, Pastor Smith. I'm so excited! And please tell your wife those decorations are exactly what I wanted," said Maya as she left the pastor's office.

She almost skipped to her candy-red Mercedes after seeing the beautiful chapel. She put on her Prada shades and opened up her sunroof. She was in such a great mood that she didn't notice her cell phone ringing. Instead, she turned up Beyonce's "Put a Ring on It" and sped off.

With the wind on her face, she thought about how jealous Toni would be once she found out that Maya and Steven would be spending their honeymoon in the Cayman Islands. She recalled Toni telling her years ago that she'd always heard that place was beautiful. She'd said she would give anything to pack up and go one day. Maya felt a tinge of sadness for her friend, so she decided to play it off as Steven's idea, even though she would love every second of telling Toni about it.

When she reached a red light, she decided to call the caterer to confirm their appointment. She turned her radio down and reached for her cell phone. "Four missed calls? What in the hell is going on?" she said aloud. All of the calls were from Toni. She shook her head as she dialed her friend's number.

"Hi Toni! I was at the chapel finalizing paperwork when you called. *Girl,* the chapel is absolutely beautiful. I could not believe that coordinator was going to have us get married at the Birmingham Jefferson Conferance Center. That's so not what we wanted. You know I like elegance and class. Nothing says that like a quaint wedding chapel with large stained glass windows and large ceilings. I probably need to call her back to schedule a run-through of how I want the ceremony to flow. Anyways, what's up girl?" she asked.

"Hey, I'm fine, and how are you?" Toni asked sarcastically. It simply amazed her how Maya would skip the pleasantries and get started on herself without as much as a "How are you doing today?"

"I just told you I was good. I'm just ready to get this wedding over so that I can relax. All of this back and forth is driving me crazy. I shouldn't have fired our wedding coordinator. It would be much better to let her handle all of this. I see why brides get them now. I need to be at the spa somewhere instead of running around with this wedding stuff. It's not like I can't afford a coordinator, but it's too late to hire someone now. I might as well deal with it," she answered, not giving a thought to the significance of Toni's sarcasm.

"Okay, I was calling you from the dress store. My dress doesn't fit. I'm going to contact my seamstress to see if she can let it out a little." Toni sounded disappointed.

"Damn, girl! I told you to stop cooking those soul food meals for Ty, especially the last few weeks before my wedding. I'm going to have to give you my recipe book. It has lots of healthy eating ideas for you. I'm sure you have the time, since you don't work." Maya stated bluntly.

"Don't worry about it. Ty loves soul food, and I don't mind cooking it for my husband. And actually, I do work. I work to make sure my husband and daughter have a comfortable life. That's a twenty-four-hour job, honey," said Toni. She usually didn't throw any shade back at Maya, but the guilt trip was starting to wear thin, and so was her patience.

"Girl, that little house don't need too much. But actually, our new house is so big I'm probably going to have to hire a maid or two. Are you interested in applying? But anyways, call me as soon as you get an answer from your seamstress. The last thing I need is my matron of honor spilling out of her dress, destroying my wedding pics. Keep me posted," said Maya. And with that, she hung up her phone without even waiting for a good-bye and called the caterer.

Once she hung up with the caterer, Maya turned up her radio and starting laughing uncontrollably. She thought, *Ty messed up big time, leaving me for Toni. She don't have nothing to do during the day and still can't find time to work out; so sad.*

She pulled into one of the open parking spaces and examined the menu she had written. Everything was going to be so perfect. She had a menu that was sure to please the most exacting palates. As Maya stepped out of her car, she was greeted by her caterer, Maxine.

Maxine was a short, heavyset lady. She wore her salt-and-pepper hair in a neat Afro. She kind of reminded Maya of the character Florida Evans on the television show *Good Times*. Maxine looked just like her, aside from the gap in Florida's teeth.

After some brief pleasantries, Maya and Maxine walked into the beautiful catering building. The space was not huge, but it was professionally decorated. The meeting room had black-and-white checkered floors, and the round tables also were decorated in black and white. Red roses popped in various vases throughout the room. The room smelled so good. It reminded Maya of Tao, a Thai restaurant in the Venetian Hotel in Las Vegas. Tao had beautiful tubs filled with rose petals and candles on both sides of the entrance. It created the greatest ambiance. And the smell was delectable.

"Now, I don't know if I have to tell you this, but the food for my wedding has to be absolutely perfect, Maxine. Remember, I'm marrying an attorney, and I'll sue your ass if I have to." Maya jokingly warned.

"No worries, Ms. Fisher. We are the best at what we do, and you will not be disappointed. Now, here's the first group of food samples for you. Lobster bisque soup, filet minion grilled medium, and caviar," said Maxine.

The presentation was gorgeous. The food was placed on a beautiful silver platter, each sample in its own individual dish. Each course was accented with Maxine's signature red roses.

"Yummy! You have outdone yourself, Maxine. As long as you make it like this for the actual reception, you and I will have no problems. I really hate that Steven is not here," Maya pouted in between chews.

"Steven; Steven Sims of Wilshire and Associates?" asked Maxine.

"Yes, I'm sure you've heard of him. My baby is one of their top attorneys. I'm a very lucky lady," Maya bragged.

Maxine only nodded and said she would be back with the rest of the menu samples. Maxine knew Steven, all right. She catered luncheons for Wilshire and Associates quite often. She thought back to her introduction to Steven Sims.

One afternoon, while unloading her van, Maxine saw what seemed to be two men kissing in a blue Corvette. She wasn't sure who they were, but she did notice the expensive vehicle. She continued unloading and watching. Soon, one of the men emerged and left in a truck. The other stayed behind for what seemed like an eternity. One of her coworkers came out to help her, and they both noticed the second man finally emerge from the vehicle.

Her coworker said, "Girl, that fine brother there is Steven Sims. He is one of the top attorneys here. I'd love to get me some of that."

Maxine started laughing and said, "Baby, that ain't what you want." Her coworker just laughed and walked back inside, looking puzzled. Maxine knew how important the Wilshire and Associates account was to her. She wouldn't dare let a little gossip stop her from getting her money. All it would take would be an associate hearing the banter, and her steady money would be gone. Gossip was one thing that did not belong in her business, a business she'd started from the ground up right after losing her job as a chef at Tavern on the Green, one of the city's most elegant restaurants.

Maxine returned with additional menu samples. She had a classic wedge salad with her signature red-wine vinaigrette, mashed potatoes, and baby peas. She tried to hide her sadness for the bride-to-be before her. She couldn't imagine what would be in store for her in the years to come. She thought that down-low brothers were the worst kind of men. They were the type to risk the lives of their women in order to keep their lives secret. They wanted to have their cake and eat it too. *But we all wear the masks at one time or another,* she thought. *Paul Laurence Dunbar said that best.*

"Oh my, that smells so good. What's wrong, Maxine?" asked Maya, noticing the change in her demeanor.

"Nothing is wrong. I just love to see my customers happy with the food. It is our goal to please," Maxine said while managing a smile and placing the samples in front of Maya. Everything in her wanted to tell Maya that she was making a huge mistake. But as much as she wanted to, she couldn't. One thing Maxine knew was that you cannot tell a woman in love shit. *She has to find out on her own, and even then, it may take a while for her to believe,* she thought.

"Well, I am happy. I'm sure my Steven will be also. He spoils me every chance he gets. He is definitely going to be shocked by this bill, though," Maya laughed.

Maya didn't know why she was bragging to Maxine about Steven. She usually saved the bragging until she could do it at Ty and Toni's expense. But she felt like a blushing bride that day. *There's nothing wrong with bragging on a good man,* she thought. Her Steven had been nothing but good to her. She knew that someday, she would fall in love with him. She knew that her Ty and Toni drama couldn't last forever. Maybe this was her chance at real happiness.

She thought of Ricky. He was also a really good friend. She needed to say something to him. In all of the chaos of the wedding planning, she had never officially thanked him for introducing Steven to her. She made a mental note to call him later on that day.

6

TONI

"Hi Gloria, how are you doing? I was wondering if you could help me out. My friend is getting married in a few weeks, and I desperately need my dress let out," said Toni.

Gloria confirmed that she was available, and Toni let out a sigh of relief after she hung up the phone. Her first thought was to call Maya, but she quickly forced it out of her mind. She started feeling down on herself as Jill Scott's vocals of "He Loves Me" played through her speakers. Toni had a degree in finance but was a home-maker. Although she loved being a stay-at-home mom, she felt as if her life was missing something.

All these years, she had watched Maya receive count-less awards and recognition. The only recognition she received was on Mother's Day. Her life revolved around PTA meetings, cleaning up behind everyone, and being a supportive wife. She supported Ty in everything he did. She had always been his cheerleader. One day, she had an epiphany. It finally occurred to her that she did all those things to prove to Ty that she was the better woman. This epiphany hit her like a ton of bricks. No wonder they rarely had arguments; she had allowed herself to become enthralled in pleasing him.

For example, Ty had chosen the house they'd bought. Toni didn't like the area, let alone the house, but she had said nothing. She had no voice. She felt as if she didn't have a choice, since she didn't work.

She knew that she was the one who had come on to Ty that day. She had wanted him even though he'd belonged to someone else. Someone else who was her friend. Now that bitch karma was showing her nasty head. She was paying for betraying her friend. Sure, she'd gotten the man in the end, but she'd lost herself.

When Ty told her that she didn't have to work, initially she'd been ecstatic. It never dawned on her that her days would be spent waiting on everyone hand and foot. Toni was up before dawn, making breakfast and ironing clothes, then wouldn't get to bed until after everyone else was asleep. Day in and day out, it was the same routine. She never had anything exciting to talk about. She found herself waiting for her family to return home so she could ask them about their day.

She didn't want to admit it, but she wasn't so sure she was happily married. She was more like happily subservient. She *appeared* happy to others. She wondered if Ty picked up on her guilt and was using it against her somehow. She shook off that thought. She knew Ty loved her.

He provided a comfortable life. She didn't have the best of things, but she didn't have the worst, either. One thing for sure was that she never wanted for anything. She didn't have expensive tastes like Maya. Labels didn't define her self-worth, and she was proud of that.

She remembered Maya's reaction when she saw the Prada bag Ty had given Toni for their third wedding anniversary. Maya had said, "And what do we have here? I know that can't be a real Prada. That must be a Nada, if you're carrying it."

Toni said, "Actually, it is real, and my husband bought it for our anniversary. He's so sweet to me."

She knew how to shut Maya down. At the time, Maya didn't even have a man. But it had hurt Toni's feelings. She couldn't understand why, but it was as if the best wasn't good enough for her. In a twisted way, Toni felt like she hadn't been able to get her own man. She'd had to settle for leftovers.

As Toni pulled into Gloria's Alteration shop, she turned down her radio and called Ty. He didn't answer. She had forgotten that he was getting together with Ricky that afternoon. *They are probably out playing pool or something,* she thought.

Grabbing the dress from the backseat, she paused to take a look at herself in the mirror on the visor. She hadn't paid too much attention to her appearance lately, but she saw that she was beautiful. She wasn't perfect, but she had a good heart. She was a great mom and had a loving, supportive husband. There was no way she was going to let

Maya or those inadequate thoughts make her hang her head down.

Hell, it isn't like Maya and Ty were ever married. It isn't like I broke up a happy home. And how happy was the home if he allowed me to have him the first chance he got? she thought.

Those thoughts had gotten Toni through a lot of self-doubt over the years. She felt like number two at times. She felt as if she couldn't compare to Maya.

As she closed the door, she held her head up high and exhaled. "I'm going to slay this dress and make Steven want me, too," she said as she sashayed toward the shop.

7

TY

The drive home was a long one. Ty weaved in and out of traffic, blasting Tupac's "All Eyez on Me" through his speakers. He was in such shock that he didn't even notice the blue lights behind him. He sped through a yellow light, then he finally saw the lights. *Damn!* he thought as he slowed down and pulled over at a nearby gas station. He turned down his radio and reached for his license and registration.

The cop was a young black male. He looked like he had just graduated from the police academy. He walked over and asked Ty what his hurry was. Ty looked at him and just shook his head, saying, "Man, you wouldn't believe me if I told you. How fast was I going?"

The officer said, "You were going fifty-three in a thirty-five zone. May I have your license and registration?" Ty cooperated and handed the officer what he'd requested.

The officer walked back to his vehicle to check to see if Ty had any warrants out on him.

Ty checked his phone and notice he had a missed call from Toni. He wanted to call her back, but he couldn't talk to anyone right now. His focus was on his friends. So many thoughts, different situations and instances ran through his mind. How in the world could he have missed the signs? There had to be obvious signs somewhere. And then he thought about poor Maya. Here this girl was about to marry this guy, and he was gay—and fucking Ricky, no less. Ty covered his mouth as the police officer walked back over.

"Mr. Weeks, I'm letting you off with a warning. You haven't had a ticket in over ten years. It's pretty obvious that something is weighing heavy on your mind, man. Try to slow it down, though. Whatever it is, it isn't worth risking your life or the lives of others," said the officer.

"Thanks a lot, man," said Ty, relieved as hell. The last thing he needed was one more bill to pay. Things were tight enough around the house. He loved Toni, but there definitely were days he wished she worked. Two incomes were always better than one. He'd never tell her that, though. As far as she knew, they were fine, and he was going to keep it that way.

The officer's words played over and over in his mind. *Whatever it is, it isn't worth risking your life or the lives of others*, he thought. That was not the case. This newfound knowledge was risking his life and the lives of others. His friend's life lay in the balance.

Ty tried to drive off, but he couldn't. He cut off the ignition and sat there. He was trying to wrap his mind around even letting on that he knew. He didn't know if he should just keep quiet or confront Steven. He knew there was no way he was going to be able to stand there while Maya made the biggest mistake of her life. He'd known her long enough to owe her the truth.

The truth is one of the most needed and dreaded things in the world. We all want it, but oftentimes can't handle it. He wondered if Maya was better off not knowing. She'd waited to become someone's wife for so long. Ty shook his head as if he had received an epiphany. Maybe that was the reason Ricky's wife had left him. It would make sense, because everything had seemed as if it was going great for them. He thought about reaching out to Laila but quickly dismissed that notion, since he wasn't sure she knew. Plus, he didn't care too much for Laila after the way she'd left his friend.

He thought about telling Toni. But he didn't trust her reaction. She'd probably never let him live it down for not telling Maya. This was going to be one of the hardest decisions he would have to make. If Toni knew about Steven, she wouldn't dare let her friend go through with the wedding.

Then he thought about just telling Maya. He knew she would have to believe him. He couldn't think of a reason why she wouldn't believe him. But he knew she would just tell Toni and make it seem like he was trying to keep her from being happy. Even though that was far from the truth, he didn't want to risk Maya thinking he wanted her in the least.

The beeping of his phone snapped him out of his trance. It was Ricky's beep. He looked down at his phone and saw that there was an apologetic message from his friend. Ricky said that he was just getting back in town and was sorry he had missed Ty's calls and texts. He said that he would be at the fitting tomorrow and that they could catch up then. The message continued with Ricky saying that he was tired and was just going to call it a night.

Ty didn't respond. He couldn't respond. His best friend had been lying to him all of these years and was lying now. He was unsure who he was actually dealing with. Ty had never been homophobic. He had nothing against people being gay. But he had a problem with liars, especially ones he called friends. He kept wondering, *Why in the hell would Ricky bother introducing Maya to Steven at all?*

One thing for sure was that he needed to go back to Ricky's house. He had to deal with this shit today. There was no way he was going through with this wedding unless he got to the bottom of this newfound information. Ty silently prayed that his friend would be honest with him and that Steven had left. He didn't want to confront the two of them together. He didn't know Steven well enough.

He cranked up his car and sped off. He prayed that he would be able to handle any truths that would come out that night. Ricky was his friend, and Ty wanted him to be honest with him without him having to ask.

8

RICKY

Ricky decided to join Steven in the shower. Nothing was sexier to him than seeing water cascade off of Steven's six-pack. Steven was just about to cut off the water when he saw his lover. He licked his lips in anticipation of the up-coming sex. He grabbed a loofah and began to lather it up with soap. Before he could begin washing his lover, they engaged in a long, passionate kiss. Steven loved to feel Ricky's member grow hard with anticipation for him. After their kiss, Steven began washing his lover. He carefully scrubbed him all over his body, then stepped out after he was done.

When Ricky was done rinsing off, Steven was waiting for him to get out of the shower. He gently dried off his lover. Once he was on his knees, he decided to stay there. He began licking Ricky in places Maya wouldn't believe his tongue would ever venture. Ricky was his little secret, and what she didn't know wouldn't hurt her. He loved her, but there was no comparison to his love for Ricky.

The two of them began making love on the bathroom floor. The wet mat provided additional support for Steven from Ricky's thrusts. He loved every inch of his lover. Ricky could make him orgasm in ways he never could with women.

Ricky began kissing, then sucking the back of Steven's neck. Steven was so caught up in pleasure that he didn't even notice that the kisses were turning into sucking. Ricky knew exactly what he was doing. He planned on leaving a hickey on Steven in hopes that Maya would notice. Maybe Steven would confess and end this whole marriage charade once and for all. Steven felt so good. Ricky loved to hear his moans and imagined them on nights when he was alone.

As Steven collapsed in ecstasy from his second orgasm, the men heard what sounded like knocking on the door. Ricky got up from behind his lover and quickly ran to the bedroom window to see Ty's car out front.

"Fuck! It's Ty. Hurry up and get dressed, man!" Ricky yelled. Steven did as he was told, threw on his clothes, and headed to the front door. Ricky quickly grabbed his clothes and ran to the bathroom to turn on the shower. He was shocked, to say the least. Ty never just showed up like this. *What in the hell is up with him, pulling some shit like this*? he thought.

After several knocks and doorbell rings, Steven calmly opened the door for Ty. "Hey man! How are you doing?"

Steven asked as he held his hand out for a handshake. Ty just stood there in disgust. He'd figured out, once he saw Steven's car, that instead of asking Ricky about what was going on, he would just have to confront them both. Ty stepped through the door, walking past Steven, and started yelling out Ricky's name.

"Is everything okay, Ty? What's going on?" Steven asked as he closed the door and followed Ty into Ricky's room, looking confused. Ty continued to ignore Steven and began banging on the bathroom door. He could smell the fresh sex in the air and almost vomited again, thinking of the scene he had just interrupted.

"Ricky, I need to talk to you now, man! Open the door!" Ty yelled. Ricky finally cut off the shower and yelled that he'd be out in a minute. Steven stood in the doorway with his arms folded. He didn't understand what the hell was going on, but he definitely did not like the fact that Ty was completely ignoring him. They had always been cool in the past, so this side of Ty was all new to him. He could feel his temper beginning to flare up.

Ricky opened the door, fully dressed. Ty stood there in complete silence as he looked at what he had thought was his best friend. "Ty, what in the hell is going on? Is everything all right with Toni?" asked Ricky.

"Ricky, what in the hell are you doing, man?" Ty asked, looking back and forth between him and Steven.

"What are you talking about, Ty?" asked Ricky, looking puzzled as hell.

"So you are going to stand there in my face and act like I don't know about you and Steven? Is that it? You are going to act like I didn't see you two grown motherfuckers kissing? What the fuck is wrong with you, man? Is he the reason Laila left? Is he?" Ty asked.

Ricky was completely dumbfounded. He stood there in a trance, not knowing what to do or say. Before he could react, Steven ran up behind Ty and hit him over the back of the head with the lamp that stood beside the bedroom door.

Blood splashed onto the bed and floor as Ty fell over. Steven hit him again before Ricky ran over to grab his hands. "What are you doing Steven? Why did you do that? Ty, Ty, are you okay, man?" he asked as he got down to check on his friend. "Call an ambulance! Call an ambulance, dammit!" Ricky yelled.

Steven just stood there. He couldn't believe what he had just done, but he knew that Ty had to be stopped. He wasn't going to let Ty destroy his relationships with Ricky and Maya. Not only that, but he had his job and reputation to think about also. Nobody was going to ruin that, not even his lover's best friend.

Just then, Ricky's phone began to ring. Ricky didn't notice because he was too busy trying to check Ty's pulse. "Ty, Ty, wake up, man!" Ricky continued. He was crying at this point.

Steven began pulling Ricky away from Ty. "Get out of here, Ricky! Take your phone and leave. I'll take care of this," Steven instructed him.

"Steven, have you fucking lost your mind? What in the fuck is wrong with you? Are you fucking crazy? How could you do that? Call the ambulance now!" Ricky cried.

"Do you want me to go to jail? Is that it? Do you want us to lose everything because of this ungrateful mother-fucker? He still has a thing for Maya, and this would be his golden ticket to destroy her happiness. He doesn't want her to be happy. He wants her to just continue to pine over his ass," exclaimed Steven.

"Man, Ty doesn't want Maya! That shit with them happened years ago. This man is somebody's husband and father. Are you fucking losing your mind? This is my best friend. Help me, please! Call the ambulance!" Ricky pleaded.

The blood began to gush out of Ty's head. He still had a slight pulse and was drifting in and out of conscientious-ness. He could hear the two men arguing about him. All he could think to do was just try to hold on. He felt the warm blood on his face and knew that this might be the end for him. If only he'd have gone home, like he'd started to do.

"Ricky, calm down and just think for a second, okay? Think about us. Think about what would happen if Ty wakes up. I can't go to jail. Think about Maya," Steven pleaded.

"Fuck Maya! You think I give a fuck about Maya knowing about us? My wife found out, and I didn't kill the bitch, Steven! I'm calling the fucking ambulance," said Ricky.

He grabbed his phone with blood-splattered hands, not noticing that it was ringing, and tried to dial, but then he heard Maya on the other end.

9

MAYA

"Hello? Ricky is that you?" Maya asked. She had been trying to call him for a few minutes. Strangely enough, he hadn't answered. "Ricky, are you okay? It's Maya," she said.

Ricky held the phone, not knowing if he should hang up or play it off. But before he could do anything, Steven shouted, "Put down the fucking phone." Ricky hung up.

"Ricky? Steven? What in the hell?" Maya yelled into the phone, puzzled. Then the phone was hung up. She didn't know what to think. She knew she wasn't crazy. The man in the background had sounded just like Steven. *But what would Steven be doing at Ricky's house?* she thought. She tried calling back, but this time it went straight to voice mail. She hung up and dialed again; same thing.

Confused as to what to do, she dialed Steven. Although his phone rang, it eventually went to voice mail. Maya decided against leaving a message on either phone number. She pulled over at a gas station to collect her thoughts. She replayed what she'd heard over and over. She couldn't understand what could possibly be going on. She knew that Steven was out of town. Was Ricky with him? If he was, why hadn't he told her? And why had Ricky answered and then hung up? All of these thoughts led Maya to try calling Ty. Maybe he knew what was going on and could put her mind at ease.

She dialed Ty's number. No answer. She was starting to worry now. Things were just not adding up. She checked her messages and e-mail to see if she'd missed something from Steven. *Maybe he told me Ricky was going with him*, she thought. *But why the hell was he screaming and cursing at Ricky? This just isn't making any sense.*

She sped out of the gas station parking lot and dialed Toni. *Maybe she has heard or knows something*, she thought.

"Toni, this is Maya. Please call me as soon as you get this message. It's important, girl," she said on the voice mail. No one wanted to answer her calls, and she had no idea why.

Maya looked at her watch. It was 4:30 p.m., and the traffic was beginning to get heavy. She was closer to Toni's house than her condo, so she decided to stop by there to see if Toni was home or to wait for her. She knew that Toni picked her daughter up from school and would be arriving home soon to get dinner started for Ty.

While she waited, she kept calling all three men. No answer from anyone. She kept replaying the events that had just transpired. She had no explanation for what had just taken place. All she knew was that shit was not adding up, and she had to get to the bottom of it.

She pulled up Facebook on her phone and typed in Steven's name. She checked to see if he had updated his status or checked in somewhere else. His last post was earlier that morning, a selfie that already had over two hundred likes. She smiled at her hubby-to-be. He was so damn handsome and accomplished. She quickly snapped out of her trance, though. After liking his picture, she clicked on it to see if he'd replied to any of the fifty comments. He hadn't replied to any of them. Then something caught her eye. It was Ricky's picture with a comment of a thumbs-up emoji.

She didn't think too much of it, but clicked on Ricky's picture to go to his profile. He hadn't updated his status, but something she saw caused her to gasp. She clicked back to Steven's selfie, then back to Ricky's profile picture. The wall behind both of them had their school mascot in the background.

10

TONI

"Sit down back there, baby. We're almost home," Toni said. She hadn't expected to be at the seamstress's that long, but she had gotten her dress fixed. She had already put her roast in the Crock-Pot, so she wasn't in that big of a hurry to get home. Instead, she talked to her daughter about her day and took the back roads home. She didn't feel like dealing with the crazy 65 South interstate.

As she settled in for the drive, she decided to see if Ty had returned her call. "Missed calls from Maya and a voice mail. What in the world does she want now?" Toni huffed. She decided against listening to the voice mail and called Maya.

She answered on the first ring. "Hello, where are you?" Maya sounded panicked.

"Hi, I'm about fifteen minutes from my house. What's up?" Toni asked.

"Have you heard from Ty or Ricky? I'm sitting here outside your house now," Maya said.

"I haven't heard from Ty since this morning. He is supposed to be catching up with Ricky tonight. Why? And why are you sitting outside of my house?" Toni asked.

"I'll tell you when you get here. Can you call your neighbor Carol and ask her to watch the baby?" Maya said.

"Maya, she's hardly a baby. Jessica is five years old now. You'd know that if you bothered to spend time with her. Anyway, why am I asking Carol to watch my daughter?" Toni was getting confused and upset by the conversation. She wanted to know what in the hell was going on, and wanted to know before she involved someone else.

"We need to talk and go see if we can find Ty and Ricky. I don't know what is going on, but something is not right. Have you heard from Ty?" Maya asked, ignoring the comment about Jessica. She knew that she wasn't a good godmother. She had purposely booked a cruise around the time of Maya's due date. She didn't know why, but she despised the little girl. Maybe it was because Jessica was the little girl she'd always wanted.

"No, I haven't. I tried calling him earlier. Just try to calm down. I'm on my way; just hang tight. I'm about ten minutes away." Toni hung up the phone and called Ty. He didn't answer. Then she called Ricky; same thing. She was starting to get worried and regretted taking the long way home.

She called her neighbor Carol, told her what was going on, and asked if she could watch Jessica for a few hours. Carol said yes. She was a retired lady who lived across the street with her husband. She had older kids, but had made sure to let Toni know that she'd been young once and that anytime Toni needed her to help with the baby, she would be glad to. Toni and Ty's parents both lived hours away.

Toni had been hesitant at first, being a first-time mommy and all. But Carol had ended up being the blessing she needed for date nights and an occasional girl's night out.

After hanging up with Carol, Toni called Ty again, this time leaving a voice mail. "Ty, call me back as soon as you get this. I don't know what in the hell is going on, but Maya is at our house, and we are headed that way. And is Ricky with you? Please call me back!"

Toni hung up as she pulled into her driveway. Maya was parked next to the mailbox. Toni grabbed her daughter and went into the house to pack her an overnight bag just in case they were out late. She knew that Carol was old-fashioned, like Toni's grandmother, and if it got too late, she would give Jessica a bath and put her to bed. She rushed around the house, grabbing this and that, then turned off her roast and headed for the door.

She waved at Maya as she walked across the street. Carol was at the door as soon as she rang the doorbell. "Hi Toni! How's my little girl?" she asked as she smiled, grabbing Jessica's tiny hands and the bag from Toni.

"Hi Carol! She's fine. I just picked her up from school. How are you doing?" asked Toni.

"Child, I'm good as long as I'm on this side of the dirt," Carol chuckled. She always had a way of reminding Toni of her grandmother.

"I guess I can't argue with that. I'll be back as soon as I can," Toni said.

"Has this baby eaten?" asked Carol.

"No, I was going to finish dinner when I got home," Toni replied as she kissed her daughter's cheek.

"Okay, I'll fix her something, then. Go on, now. She's going to be just fine." Carol smiled and closed the door.

Toni smiled too. She felt a sense of relief at having someone whom she could trust with her daughter. Jessica loved Carol too, probably because she made her homemade cookies and pastries all the time. Maya never had time to babysit. To hear her tell it, she was always going out or was too busy with work. *Some godmother*, Toni thought. Maya didn't even get around to seeing Jessica until she was six weeks old. A sudden trip to Italy had happened to come up, and Maya just could not turn it down.

Toni walked over to Maya's car and got in on the passenger's side. "Girl, what in the hell is going on? I called Ty and Ricky, and they didn't answer for me either," Toni said.

"Okay, Steven is supposed to be out of town. I called Ricky to thank him for introducing us and everything. You know we haven't really been on good terms since I went off on Laila's ass. Then he answers his phone, and I hear what sounds like Steven in the background telling him to hang up the fucking phone," Maya blurted.

Toni gasped. "What in the world?"

"It gets worse," Maya continued. "I call back, and it keeps going to voice mail. I call Steven, and his phone just rings and rings. So I pull up Facebook, and Steven's selfie that he took this morning has the mascot from our college in the background. Now look at Ricky's profile picture." She handed Toni her phone.

"What the fuck?" Toni asked.

"Same damn thing I said. Something is definitely not right. Do you think he has another woman and Ricky is covering for him?" Maya asked as she drove out of Toni's neighborhood.

"Girl, I doubt it. Steven loves you. And I sure as hell hope Ty and Ricky ain't involved in trying to help him if he is cheating. He just doesn't seem like that type of guy," Toni reassured her.

"Toni, I don't know what to think. I mean, it's not like I haven't been through betrayal and bullshit like this before though," Maya said as she pulled onto the interstate.

"There has to be an explanation, Maya. Just calm down. We'll get to the bottom of it. Take the next exit," Toni instructed.

Toni acted as if she didn't hear Maya's comment Maya. That had been her norm all these years anyway. She wasn't sure why she was even still friends with Maya. There hadn't been a genuine friendship between the two of them since Ty. She couldn't think of a time Maya had actually been there for her in years; now here Toni was, dropping everything for her yet again.

Instead of commenting, Toni just sat there staring out of the window into the sunset. Oddly enough, it was the first time she'd seen the sun set in months. She marveled at God and all of his artistry. She secretly thanked Maya for that simple experience and hoped that one day she would be able to return the favor.

11

TY

The night should have been filled with brews and pool cues. It should have been filled with laughter from reminiscing about old times. Ty missed his friend. So much had happened the last few months, and he needed to get back to where they once were.

Ty had been drifting in an out of conscientiousness. He didn't know where he was, but he was not on the floor of Ricky's bedroom anymore. He remembered being picked up but he wasn't conscious enough to know by who.

All he had was regret. He knew that he should have just gone home. He wondered how in the hell he'd gotten caught up in this bullshit. He'd thought about heading back home when he saw Steve's car, but the dedication he had to Maya and Ricky had made him do otherwise.

His disgust had grown as he'd gotten out of his car and headed to the door. He'd just kept thinking that he was not in the right frame of mind to handle the conversation that day. Regret was no longer going to be his excuse.

He did know that Steven had hit him and that Ricky had tried to get him help. He'd heard screaming and yelling from both men. He remembered Steven telling Ricky to leave and that he would take care of it. *Was it him?* he thought.

Ty opened his eyes to total darkness. He began looking around to see where he was. The space was definitely small. He was balled up in something and could barely breathe. Then he heard a car door slam and an engine start up. He began to move. *I must be in the trunk of a car,* he thought.

He tried to concentrate on the direction he was moving. He knew that they must have been on a back road, because the exit to the interstate was not far from Ricky's house. There were no sounds of traffic. The road was bumpy at times. He tried listening to what sounded like someone talking, but the voice was muffled. Wherever he was headed, it sure as hell was not the hospital.

Ty knew he had to remain calm. The last thing he needed was to start hyperventilating or pass out again. He knew he was going to be in the fight of his life and needed to conserve what little energy he had left. His head was pounding, and he could feel wetness all around his face. He passed out again.

When he woke up again, the car was no longer moving. The engine was no longer running either. He heard people and cars in the background. It sounded like he was in a parking lot or something. He began yelling as loud as he could, and got one arm free and started beating on the trunk for what seemed like an eternity.

"Hello? Is somebody in there?" an unfamiliar voice called to him.

"Yes! I've been attacked. Get me out of here! Please help me! Help!" Ty screamed.

"Don't worry, buddy. I'm calling the police. Bill, get something to break the damn window. We need to get him out of there now!" the unknown man yelled.

Ty heard the window break and felt the car moving. He tried to hold on and answer the questions the guy was asking. The guy told him that his friend was looking for the trunk button and that help was on the way. He asked Ty where was he hurt.

Before Ty could respond, he lost consciousness again.

12

RICKY

Blood was everywhere. Beads of sweat dripped down Ricky's face as he mopped his bedroom floor. His heart was racing at what felt like a thousand beats a minute. He was crying as he tried to rehearse what he would say to Toni. Deep down, he felt remorse. If Steven hadn't taken his phone, he probably would have called the police.

"Now I'm a fucking accessory to murder. My God, Ty, why in the hell did you come over here? Damn, you were my best friend! What have we done?" he cried.

In all the chaos, he'd forgotten to tell Steven about Maya's call. He was not sure if he'd hung up before or after Steven had yelled at him. Steven had grabbed Ricky's phone and put it in his pocket before Ricky could do or say anything.

He picked up the broken lamp, wrapped it in a trash bag, and placed it in the trash can behind his house, as Steven had instructed. He then went back to his bedroom and began scrubbing the walls. The clean-up was quickly done, but it felt like hours to Ricky.

Ricky peeled off his bloodstained clothes and placed them in a bag. He had to quickly shower and leave. He and Steven had decided it would be best if they stayed at the Hamilton Hotel that night. Steven was going to get a cab to take him there.

The story would be that he had simply never seen Ty. They didn't have plans to meet that night, so technically, there would be no way to prove that Ricky was even there. His story would be that he'd texted Ty and Ty had never re-plied. Steven told him that as long as he stuck to the story, he would be fine.

Steven's alibi was solid as well. His firm did have him booked at the seminar, so as far as anyone else knew, he was not even in the city. Being an attorney, Steven was quick to think of every scenario that might possibly play out.

Ricky replayed the events as the hot water hit his face. Steven had taken off Ty's watch and wedding ring. He'd also removed Ty's wallet from his back pocket. He had then rolled Ty up in the comforter from Ricky's bed. He had instructed Ricky to put on gloves and pull Ty's car into the garage. Once it was in the garage, Steven had removed everything from Ty's car. He'd also taken off the license plate and scratched out the vehicle identification number near the dashboard. When he was done, he and Ricky had picked Ty up and placed him in the trunk.

Steven was going to drive Ty about thirty minutes west, near his home, and leave the car in the Target parking lot.

Ty would be a robbery victim. Someone had seen him, robbed him, and left him for dead.

Ricky turned off the shower and walked over to the mirror in front of his sink. He wiped off the steam to reveal a shaken man. His eyes were empty. His face was hollow-looking, as if he'd seen a ghost. He dropped his head in shame. He'd been so selfish. *How in the hell am I going to muster up enough courage to tell Toni these lies?* he thought. *And when Ty is found, how can I even think about attending the funeral?* A million thoughts ran through his mind as he dried off.

The tears were a different story. His eyes seemed to not care that he was trying to calm down. They refused to forget what they had just witnessed. Their only way of coping was to run like faucets. The tears of the real Ricky ran down his face, not the man Steven had turned him into within the blink of an eye.

Ricky didn't want this to happen. He wanted to call an ambulance and the police. He knew that Ty wasn't dead yet. There was still time to save him. Still time to prove that Ricky wasn't this monster. Still time to be the man and best friend he appeared to be. Still time to act like a human being.

But his lover was right. There would be no way to explain what had happened. No way to explain that they were being confronted by Ricky's best friend about their sexual relationship. No way to tell Maya the truth without revealing theirs. There simply was no other way. At least, that was the story that Steven had convinced him to believe.

Ricky quickly dressed in a blue sweat suit and grabbed the bloody bag of clothes. Steven had told him that he needed to ditch them away from the house. He grabbed Steven's luggage bag and hurried out the door to Steven's car.

13

MAYA

Maya's mind ran a mile a minute as she swerved in and out of traffic. In her panic, she had forgotten that Ricky lived over two hours away. "No wonder Steven was 'away on business.' He was away at Ricky's house, fucking some tramp!" she screamed. "Damn, how could I have been so naïve? I'll bet it is that new client of his."

"What new client?" Toni asked, filing her nails and not really giving a damn.

"The bitch I was telling you about a few weeks ago, Kitty Washington. She's the real estate broker being sued by my company. She knows I can't stand her big titty ass ever since she stole my client. That bitch cost me over thirty thousand in commission, and now she has the nerve to take my man," Maya huffed.

"Look, you don't know that to be true. We don't know anything to be true other than everyone has gone ghost, and you heard what may have been Steven in the background," Toni stated mater of factly as she checked her phone for messages.

"Well, how do you explain what sounded like Steven yelling at Ricky when his ass is supposed to be away on business? How do you explain the same fucking background in the pictures on Facebook? " Maya asked.

"He could have taken that picture months ago. Just because it was a recent post on Facebook doesn't mean the actual picture was taken today. Don't you trust him, Maya? Damn, you are about to marry this man, and now we're headed down the highway acting like Thelma and Louise." Toni burst out laughing as she flashed back to one of her favorite movies. She made a mental note to watch it later tonight with Ty. She loved their impromptu movie nights. Ty would stay up watching no matter how long the movie was. They'd pig out on snacks and usually fall asleep in each other's arms.

Maya ignored Toni and turned up her radio. She needed to hear Beyonce's vocals right about now. Toni's calmness was starting to get on her nerves. Maya now hated that she had brought Toni. If she did catch Steven with a woman, there went her perfect relationship and dream wedding, and Toni would have front-row seats to its destruction.

Maya couldn't let that happen. She had come too close to beating Ty and Toni to have it blow up in her face like this. The house sale had been finalized, and the honeymoon and everything else was planned out just like she wanted.

She looked at her watch and saw that they had only been on the road for an hour. She had to come up with a way to go on alone. Her wedding was a few weeks away, and she was not going to let anyone fuck it up. She would have to deal with Steven her own way. And that way could not involve Toni.

She grabbed her phone and sent a text to her assistant telling her to call her in exactly ten minutes. "Girl, I really don't know why I'm bugging out like this. I'm sure there is a perfectly good explanation. Steven loves me. Maybe it's this wedding stuff that has me on edge," she lied as she turned down the radio to make sure that Toni would hear her phone ring.

"Maybe so, Maya. You have to trust the one lying beside you, even if you don't trust anyone else," said Toni.

Just then, Maya's phone rang, and she acted as if it was the last thing she was expecting to hear. "Steven! Where are you? Okay, so why haven't you been answering my calls? Yeah, well, do you have any idea how worried I was? Okay, baby. Well, I'm driving, so I'll call you back when I make it home. Love you, too. Bye now," she said. She hung up and immediately texted her assistant to say thanks.

"So where is he, Maya?" Toni asked.

"Girl, he's been in a conference all day. He said that he didn't have reception in the meeting room. God, I feel like such an idiot," Maya said, managing to have a look of relief on her face.

"Thank God! See, I told you there was nothing to worry about. You can't jump the gun on your man without speaking to him first. I love you, but I really didn't feel like playing *The First 48* with your ass tonight," laughed Toni.

"Yeah, you know, you're absolutely right. I have a good man. Guess I haven't had a good one in so long that I forgot what one feels like." Maya smiled as she took the next exit to turn around.

She was relieved that she had successfully completed her impromptu plan. The very thought of Toni witnessing her love life go up in flames once again was too much to bear. She mentally checked the list in her head that she'd beaten Toni again.

14

TONI

As the vocals of Lauryn Hill and D'Angelo's "Nothing Even Matters" filled the car, Toni thought back to the night Ty had proposed to her.

It was their senior year in college. They hadn't spent much time together the last few weeks because they were both studying for finals. Ty asked her to meet him at Vulcan Park the night after their last final. Toni was so excited to see him.

She took a long bath that night, making sure to add a capful of Avon's Skin So Soft bath oil to her water. It had been a while since they'd made love, and she wanted her skin to be extra soft for him. She put on a pink maxi dress that hugged all of her curves and a tiny pink G-string and didn't bother to wear a bra. Ty loved it when she wore stuff like that. He made it no secret that he was not only in love with her, but her body as well. Sometimes he would just stare at her naked body, and she loved letting him.

He had told her to text him when she made it to the park and said he would come get her. She did as she was told. Ty had the biggest grin on his face when he saw her.

"Hey, babe! How are you doing?" Toni asked as she grabbed her purse.

"Hey, I'm good now that you're here," he said.

He opened her car door and planted the biggest kiss on her lips. She couldn't wait for him to kiss the other set. He grabbed her hand and led her up the hill.

When they got to the top, there were candles lit on the ground, what looked like the white comforter from Ty's bed laid out, and a bouquet of pink balloons. He handed her a pink rose. The scene looked like it was out of a movie. They had a view of the whole city.

"Oh my God! Ty, this is so beautiful! To what do I owe the honor of all of this?" Toni asked, unable to stop smiling.

"I just thought that I could make a memory with you tonight. You know, something you can tell our grandkids one day. I also made you my famous spaghetti and meatballs. Here's a salad, and I even managed to steal a bottle of wine from my roommate's closet," Ty laughed as he helped her sit on a pillow.

"I don't know what to say. This is so nice. You are going to make me cry." Toni blushed.

"I don't want to make you cry, baby. I want to make you mine," he said, looking directly into her eyes. Toni was shocked by the absolute seriousness in his eyes.

"Make me yours? I thought I was already yours," she laughed.

"I mean make you officially mine," Ty said as he took a small box out of his pocket. "Toni, you have made me so happy. I have never felt this way about another woman. You always support me and I just want…Well, I want you to marry me. I can't see myself living without you." And with that, he opened the box and showed her the ring.

"Ty, I love you so much. I'd be honored," said Toni.

He took the ring out and placed it on her finger. It was a perfect fit. Toni cried, and Ty wiped her tears away so gently. She'd never been touched like that by any man.

Toni knew that Ty didn't have a lot of money, so she treasured that ring. She didn't need the carats. She needed the character of the man.

They sat at their moonlit picnic, laughing and talking all night. It was a memory that Toni would treasure as long as she lived. She believed that was the night she knew she had to be perfect going forward. He had chosen her, and there was no way she would leave him with regrets.

Toni looked down at her ring. This was the first time in years she'd thought about how beautiful her proposal had been. That was the night she had officially accepted her place in Ty's life. That ring symbolized so much more than the carats.

"Toni, Toni, Toni!" yelled Maya as she pumped gas.

"Huh?" Toni asked, snapping out of her trip down memory lane.

"Girl, where were you? I've only called your name like a thousand times," Maya said with an attitude.

"I'm sorry. My mind was somewhere else. What's up?" Toni replied.

"Well, ask your mind if she would like something out of the store," Maya asked as she put up the nozzle.

"I'm good, girl. Just ready to get home. This has been one crazy night," Toni said as she checked her phone. *Still no call from Ty. No text either,* she thought.

She called Carol and told her that she would be there to get her daughter in about twenty minutes. The memory of her proposal made her more anxious to see Ty. She wanted to see him. She needed to feel him inside her. She wanted all of her husband that night.

15

TY

"Sir, sir, can you hear me?" asked Nurse Brown. Ty didn't respond. "Sir, if you can hear me, please squeeze my hand," she continued as she held his left hand. "I'm sorry, officers. He is still out of it. We have to run some additional tests. I'll come and get you all as soon as he regains conscientiousness," she said as she wheeled him to the lab.

Ty had been unconscious since he'd arrived at the hospital. The guys who had found him in the trunk gave the officers all the information they knew, which was very little. They said that they heard noises coming from the trunk of the car but that the guy they rescued never gave a name. The officers searched Ty's car and clothing but could not find any traces of identification. They checked all local precincts to see if there was a missing person's report that matched his description. There was nothing. One officer noted that the car's identification number looked as if it had been scratched out. Even the surveillance videos from the area were cloudy.

The car was towed for additional evidence collection, but since the window was broken out on the driver's side, the police knew they would have a hard time getting accurate fingerprints.

"What do we have here?" the doctor asked as Nurse Brown wheeled Ty into the lab.

"It looks like this guy was the victim of a robbery. His head has been hit pretty hard, and he's suffered lots of blood loss," Nurse Brown stated.

"It looks like he's pretty stable now. We won't know exactly how bad this is until he regains consciousness. He's lost a lot of blood. We may have to do a transfusion, so get Matt up here so we can find out this guy's blood type. I'll get Lou Ann to stitch him up," said the doctor.

"Right away, doctor. Oh, and doctor, I noticed that he probably usually wears a ring. There's a tan line on his left finger. If he's married, this will be a tough night once his wife sees him," Nurse Brown said as she walked out, shaking her head. In her twenty years of working in the ER, she had never gotten used to the pain and hurt of the victims' loved ones.

Nurse Brown was in her late fifties and around six feet tall. She had light skin and jet-black, wavy hair. She always wore it in a high bun. Her eyes were hazel, and although she was older, she was still attractive. Her slim figure alluded to the fact that she had worked out when she was younger.

She started working on the unknown man's chart and room. She made it a point to take extraspecial care of her patients. She wasn't married and didn't have any kids or nearby relatives. She knew it was only a matter of time before she would need someone to take care of her, and hopefully God would bless her with people who cared about others just as much as she did. She believed in karma and tried to put out good vibes and positive thoughts all of the time.

She did dread the call to the man's family, though, especially his wife. She exhaled as she prepared the sheets for his room. "Be strong, young brother. I'm going to do my best to help you get through this." she whispered.

16

RICKY

The Hamilton Hotel was a staple in downtown Douglasville. It had been there for over fifty years. The outside structure was still impeccable. It had the look and feel of a huge mansion. The inside was filled with gold and red decor that made even the snooty guests gasp at its grandeur.

Ricky parked on a side of the hotel that was not as well lit as the one with the entrance. He didn't want to get out. He still wanted to call the police. He knew there was still time to save Ty.

He needed to calm himself, so he had rolled a joint on his way over. The flame from the cigarette lighter reminded him of the blood he'd just cleaned up. As he inhaled the lovely ganja, he thought of Steven. *Only love can make someone go this far,* he thought as he shook his head. The soothing sounds of Anita Baker's "Sweet Love" played softly in the background. He was in love with Steven. His mind went back to the night they had first slept together.

It was the beginning of spring, about three years ago. Ricky had to meet with some colleagues at the Tavern, a local bar in Douglasville. He'd met Steven a few weeks before and knew that he was going to be there. Ricky was looking forward to speaking with him again. The first time they'd met, Ricky was a goner. Steven was absolutely gorgeous to him. It had been a long time since he'd been attracted to another man.

When Ricky arrived at the Tavern, he immediately saw his colleagues. He knew he needed to chat it up with them so he could use the old ball and chain as an excuse to cut out early. What he really wanted to do was get better acquainted with Steven.

Steven walked in, wearing a dark blue blazer and jeans. He was magical. Ricky remembered licking his lips as Steven walked by acting as if he didn't see him.

He excused himself to go to the restroom. Steven followed a few minutes later. Although they were only acquaintances, Ricky sensed a vibe from Steven and was ready to see if the feeling was mutual.

"So we meet again," Ricky said as Steven walked into the restroom.

"It sure seems that way. Good to see you again. Are you enjoying yourself?" Steven asked, looking around the restroom to see if anyone else was in there.

"You know, it's work, so I guess I should be grateful for the opportunity. It is nice to get out of the house, though. My wife nags the absolute hell out of me," Ricky said.

"So you're married. Oh, nice ring. How long?" Steven asked.

"Yeah, about two years now. What about you? Are you seeing anyone?"

"No, I'm still looking. It's hard to find someone with my crazy schedule. I'm staying at the Hamilton, not far from here, in room three oh seven. If you want to stop by for a drink later, I'll be there," Steven said.

"Sounds good. How long are you going to be here?" Ricky asked.

"I just needed to show my face. I'm ready when you are," said Steven.

"Cool, give me about thirty minutes, and I'll meet you there."

The two said their good-byes. Ricky went back to his colleagues and watched Steven walk out of the Tavern. He had no idea what he had just agreed to do, but he knew he wanted to be alone with Steven.

After Ricky said his final good-byes, he hesitated before he typed "the Hamilton Hotel" into his GPS. He had been having so many problems with his wife that he just needed to find some peace. He'd been fighting the urge to file for divorce for some time now, but he did love Laila and thought he owed it to her to at least stick it out. Steven was something new and exciting. Even if this was a one-time thing, Ricky reasoned that it was worth it.

Ricky was in awe as he pulled into the parking lot of the Hamilton. He could see why Steven was staying there. From the outside, it reminded him of some sort of castle. He quickly parked and walked in. The place was really nice. He walked toward the elevators as if he was staying there, so he wouldn't bring attention to himself. The last thing he needed was for a colleague to see him.

After getting off on the third floor, Ricky quickly followed the signs toward room 307. Steven answered the door as soon as he knocked. He had changed into a pair of pajama pants and a T-shirt.

"Hey, come on in and make yourself at home. I'm glad you found it all right. Are you a Scotch drinker?" asked Steven.

"Not really, but hey, whatever you have is fine with me. This is a really nice room," commented Ricky.

"Thanks, I found this place a few years ago when I started my job. They have a lot of conferences in Atlanta, and I absolutely hate Atlanta. I figured this was a nice halfway point. A friend of mine suggested this place."

Ricky took a seat on the couch. The television was on, but they were not watching it. They talked about their jobs, love lives, and favorite sport teams. The conversation was very engaging. The Scotch continued to flow.

After about two hours of Steven sitting in the chair at the desk, he walked over and casually sat on the couch near Ricky. He grabbed the remote off of the nightstand and turned to another channel. Ricky was so wrapped up in their conversation about what basketball team was going to the playoffs that he didn't even notice the porn on the television. It wasn't until he heard the moans that he stopped talking to turn and see what it was.

There were two guys fucking wildly in the shower. His mouth dropped open, and his dick began to get hard. Steven inched closer to him. There was no more left to be said. He slid his hands down Ricky's pants to feel the bulge that he'd been eyeing since Ricky sat down. The two men began to kiss passionately. With Ricky's dick at full salute, Steven eagerly took all of it into his mouth.

Ricky's eyes rolled to the back of his head. Steven's head game was unlike any he'd ever received. The wetness of his mouth coupled with the extreme deep throat action caused Ricky to cum in a matter of minutes. Steven swallowed every drop of it. He was careful not to let any spill out of his mouth.

Steven wouldn't let up. He kept slurping until Ricky's member grew hard again. He pulled a condom out of his pajama pants pocket and slid it onto Ricky with his mouth. Ricky was so into it that he could barely contain himself. The two men undressed each other.

Steven guided Ricky to the extralarge walk-in shower and turned the water on, careful to not stop kissing him and to keep him in the mood. The water was hot and steamy, just like their fucking. Ricky packed Steven's every crevice. He gave it to him rough and hard, causing both of them to cum at the same time. Their orgasms were so intense that the two men collapsed on the shower floor.

They didn't speak, but rather gazed at each other. They each wondered what the other was thinking. After a few more minutes, they completed their shower, washing and kissing each other in the process.

Ricky's mind was blown. He didn't know what to do at this point. He decided the best thing to do was to end the night and head back home. He dressed quickly and thanked his lover for an awesome experience. He didn't know if he'd ever see Steven again. His emotions were so thick that he pulled over and threw up on his way home.

The urge to be with another man had subsided years ago, but he always felt the attraction. It was something about Steven, though. He revived a sexual part of Ricky that no woman could ever reach.

As the song ended in the background, Ricky finished his joint. His mind was contorted with waves of high mixed with emotion. He grabbed his bags and headed for room 307.

17

MAYA

The drive back to Toni's house seemed to take an eternity. Maya whipped in and out of traffic. Toni tuned her out as she concentrated on texting and calling Ty. Maya could sense that she was getting worried.

"Heard from Ty yet?" Maya asked, trying to act like she was concerned.

"No, and I'm getting worried. It's not like him to not text back—or call back, for that matter. Especially with it being dinnertime. You can just drop me off in front of Carol's house," Toni instructed. Clearly. her mind was off of Maya's problems and on hers.

"Okay, sorry for dragging you out all night. Tell Ty I said hello when he gets back," Maya said as Toni nodded and got out of her car.

Maya didn't even wait for Toni to get her daughter and get safely across the street. She drove off and started dialing Steven's number. She got his voice mail again. "Steven, what the hell is going on with you? I've been calling you for hours. I'm getting pissed the fuck off! Call me back as soon as you get this message!" she yelled.

She decided against going back to Ricky's house. She wasn't in the mood to drive anymore. Besides, she wasn't prepared for what she could face if he was actually there with another woman. As far as she was concerned, he could have the woman as long as her married her. That was a bit of a stretch, but that was how she felt. She didn't love Steven. She loved the opportunity he presented.

Maya couldn't believe how she'd let her emotions take over. *Of all the people to bring with me, I brought Toni. Toni, the Toni who stole the life I could be living. Toni, the one who had it all. Toni, the main one I have to constantly prove I'm better than,* she thought.

God, she thought. *How in the hell did I let this happen?*

She took the exit back onto the interstate. The traffic was flowing heavily. Unfortunately, so were Maya's tears. She pulled down the visor and exposed what she thought she'd been hiding all these years, her love for Ty. He was the cute guy who had almost bumped into her dad her first day on campus. He was the guy she'd met officially at the party their first night on campus. He was her dream. She shook her head in dismay that he hadn't chosen her. As the pain in Mary J Blige's "Be Happy" played, her mind danced back down memory lane to when she'd fallen in love with Ty.

The night Maya received the call that her dad had died had to be one of the worst nights she'd ever had to endure. Ty held her for hours.

She'd never been held like that before. He told her to let it out. She did as she was told by her love. She screamed, she yelled and cried until her eyes refused to release any more tears.

Afterward, he ran her a bubble bath and lit candles all around the tub in his apartment. He undressed her gently. Then he picked her up and carried her to the tub. He told her to relax and said that if she needed to stay in there after the water got cold, he'd run her new water. The bubbles, candles, and warm water soothed Maya's spirit. The calmness soothed her soul. The love she felt for Ty relaxed her mind. She'd finally found her king. She was officially in love with him.

After she was done with her bath, Ty came in and slowly dried her off. He dressed her in one of his big T-shirts and helped her get in bed. The sheets were fresh, as if he'd just washed them. He never spoke. He couldn't find the words to say. He knew he had to be Maya's rock. He held her all night. His arms were powerful. Being wrapped up in them gave her the comfort and strength she needed.

The next morning, he drove her to Memphis. The ride there was a mostly quiet one. He played the radio as Maya sat back and reminisced about her dad while trying to hold back the tears. She never really forgave herself for going to college before his treatment. She remembered breaking down the moment she saw her father's Jeep in the driveway. Ty pulled up and waited until she composed herself before seeing her mother. He remembered Maya telling him that she wanted to be strong for her. Her mom was going to drive her back after the funeral. She knew Ty had class. To Maya's surprise, Ty ended up staying the entire time. He told her that he wouldn't leave until she was ready to leave. He was going to be her protector now. So she thought.

Maya's tears turned into waterfalls as the radio changed songs. Maya tried wiping them away, but after her tissue was soaked, she stopped trying. She let down her window to let the wind dry her tears, but to no avail. She just had to let them out. These were tears that had built up after her meeting with Ty and Toni all those years ago. Tears she had held in as she watched Toni marry her one true love. Tears that had continued to mount after the birth of Toni and Ty's daughter.

She began to remember the humiliation and the feeling of not being good enough. The level of maturity it took for her to stand beside a woman who had stolen the love of her life was life changing. It made her bitter.

This type of hurt had turned Toni into Maya's enemy. Maya loved Toni but also hated her for what she'd taken from her. Maya had made herself think that if Ty continued to see her, he would one day come to his senses. She'd apologize to Toni but happily accept Ty back where he belonged. The tears represented Maya's white flag of surrender. She had finally realized that day would never come, and it broke her heart all over again.

18

TONI

Toni didn't eat dinner. Instead, she bathed Jessica, read her a story, and acted as if Ty would walk through the door at any minute. Deep down, the thought of not hearing from him weighed on her mind heavily.

Maya weighed on her mind too. Carol commented on the fact that Toni's *best friend* didn't bother to even get out and help her with her daughter. She said that the least Toni could have done was wait until they made it in the house safely. Toni agreed with her but didn't provide an explanation.

Lord knows it was a difficult situation to be placed in. But she always gave Maya the benefit of the doubt. Their run-in with Ricky's ex-wife Laila a few years before their sudden divorce was another example of how she defended her friend.

They were at Toni's house for the big Floyd Mayweather fight. Everyone was having a good time, sitting around drinking, eating, and laughing. Maya had arrived late, as usual, and didn't bother to speak to Laila when she came into the kitchen. Instead, she sashayed by Laila and started fixing a plate.

As the night progressed, Maya asked Laila to pass her a bottle of wine. Laila completely snapped at her. She said, "Oh, so now you see me? You've been here damn near an hour and haven't said as much as a hello and have the nerve to ask me to do something? Bitch, you have me fucked up!"

Everybody looked shocked as hell. Aside from the sounds of the TV, the whole room was quiet. Laila never really cursed, but she was so sick and tired of Maya's better-than-you attitude. She had noticed it the very first moment she'd met Maya. She barely said hello to her. She always tried to keep the peace, because they all were mutual friends, but she never was one to kiss anyone's ass.

Maya said, "Excuse me? Who the hell are you calling a bitch?" Then Toni stepped in and asked Laila and Ricky to leave. This pissed Ty off, because he knew how Maya was, and so did everybody else.

Laila grabbed her purse and walked out the door. After Ricky told Ty how fucked up it was for Toni to take Maya's side, he left too. Ty was so pissed at Toni. They ended up arguing that night. She tried, to no avail, to remind Ty that whether Maya had spoken or not, it was wrong of Laila to call her names.

That little incident caused Ricky and Ty to stop speaking for a while. Toni wished she would have let Maya fight her own battle. She actually like Laila. Laila had been there for her more during her pregnancy than Maya had been. Hell, it was Laila who had gotten together the baby shower that Maya had taken the credit for. Toni remembered Laila telling her that all Maya had done was give her some money for it. All of the planning, decorating, and inviting had come from Laila.

Snapping out of her thoughts of Maya and Laila, Toni decided to try Ty's cell again. "Ty, what in the world is going on with you? I've tried calling. I've texted over and over. Where are you? Call me now! I'm beyond worried. I love you, bye." Toni let out a deep sigh.

It was almost midnight. All she could do was pace the floor. Every time a car drove by, Toni rushed to the window. The blinds were permanently damaged at this point.

Where is my husband? she thought. *Ty has never done anything like this.* She tried Ricky again; no answer.

"Hey Ricky, it's Toni again. Listen, please call me back. If Ty is with you, tell him he needs to call home as soon as possible. The last I heard, he was going to see you today. I haven't heard from him since earlier today, and I'm worried. Call me, bye."

Toni checked her messages for what seemed like the hundredth time. She called Maya. She got her voice mail.

"Now, that's typical Maya for you. She's never available when I need her, but I always jump when she needs me," Toni huffed.

She declined to leave a voice mail and also made a mental note to ignore Maya for the next few days. She knew that despite the bullshit from earlier tonight, Maya would soon be calling to brag about something. *I'm sure Steven will send a dozen long-stemmed roses with a pink teddy bear attached to apologize for worrying her. Hell, she probably will send it for him, knowing her,* Toni thought.

She made herself sit down in Ty's recliner. She inhaled deeply. It smelled like him. She loved his cologne. She pulled a blanket close to her and waited. She waited for her phone to ring. She waited for a text message. She waited to hear the garage door open. She waited in vain.

Her worried mind told her to call the police. She quickly decided against that. Besides, she knew her husband.

Her rational mind told her that she was overreacting. *There has to be a perfectly good explanation for this. Maybe they are out at a bar or something. Maybe both of their phones died,* she thought. She had been getting on Ty lately about not keeping his phone charged.

She decided to follow her rational mind and drifted off to sleep in Ty's recliner with her cell phone in her hand.

19

TY

Nurse Brown was writing on her chart when Ty awoke. He jolted forward so quickly that she almost dropped her chart trying to restrain him.

"Calm down, sir. Please, calm down. I'll explain what has happened to you as best as I can," she said. When she felt the tension leave his body, she released her hold.

Ty looked around in a total panic. He began to realize that he was in a hospital bed. He tried to speak, but his throat was too dry. He swallowed instead and prepared to listen to the nurse over the loud sound of the heart monitor.

"My name is Nurse Brown. You were brought here several hours ago by an ambulance. You've suffered a terrible head injury and have lost a lot of blood. Can you tell me your name?" she asked.

Ty motioned to his throat. The nurse pointed to the pitcher of water next to his bed. He nodded to let her know he needed a drink. She grabbed a Styrofoam cup and straw. The sound of the water made Ty's head throb. He took a long swallow of water before releasing the straw from his mouth. After composing himself, he mumbled, "Ty, Ty Weeks."

"Ty Weeks?" she confirmed as he nodded. "Ty, I need to notify your family. Are you married?"

"I am. My wife's name is Toni. You can reach her at 205-635-7845," he said slowly.

The nurse jotted the information down on her chart. Before she could ask any more questions, two detectives walked into the room. Detectives Reed and Price had been waiting to see if Ty would regain consciousness so they could gather information to began their investigation.

Detective Reed was almost six feet tall. He looked like he frequently took advantage of the precinct's gym. He had a scruffy beard, bronzed face, and bald head. He acted as if he was the more professional one.

Detective Price reminded Ty of a good old country boy from the civil rights era. He was short and stocky. He looked unshaven, and his hair was unkempt.

"Good evening, sir. I'm Detective Reed. This is my partner, Detective Price. We've been assigned to your case. I want you to know that we plan to do all we can to find the person or persons involved in what happened to you. We'd like to ask you a few questions," Detective Reed stated.

Ty nodded but really couldn't understand why they were there. He thought that he'd been in a car accident or something. His mind was completely scrambled.

Detective Reed took out his notepad and pen. Not looking up from it, he said, "State your full name, please."

"My name is Ty Milton Weeks," Ty answered.

"Do you know who could have done this to you, Mr. Weeks?" the detective asked.

Ty looked confused. He tried to think back to his accident but couldn't remember anything about it. The last thing he remembered was getting off work the day before.

"Who did this? Didn't I get into a car accident?" Ty asked, looking from one detective to the other.

"Mr. Weeks, you were found in the trunk of a car, unconscious," said Detective Price, not hiding the fact that he'd become annoyed.

"What? Wait a minute. Are you serious? What day is it?" Ty asked.

"Today is Thursday, Mr. Weeks," said Nurse Brown. She could sense that the questioning was making her patient more uncomfortable.

Just then, the doctor came in and asked the detectives to step out while he examined Ty. The detectives looked concerned but did as they were told. They remained close enough to the door to hear the conversation.

"Good evening, I'm Doctor Jamison. How are you feeling?" the doctor asked while shining a light in Ty's eyes.

"Doctor, my head is pounding, and I don't know what is happening or what has happened," said Ty.

"Well, I've reviewed your CAT scan, and it seems that you may be suffering from temporary memory loss. Now, I'm not completely sure. We'll definitely need to run some more in-depth tests. Due to the nature of your head injury, I think I'm spot on with this, though. Do you remember anything about tonight?" he asked.

While Nurse Brown excused herself to contact Toni, Ty leaned back in his hospital bed. He was in extreme pain and shock. He tried desperately to remember what had brought him to this point. He closed his eyes and waited for recollection.

After what seemed like forever, he began to speak.

"The last thing I remember is driving home from work, and it was Wednesday," Ty said, dropping his head as if he'd been defeated.

20

RICKY

Ricky passed the familiar desk clerk at the Hamilton. He gave her a slight nod as he walked toward the elevators. He'd hoped that she wouldn't smell the marijuana on him but could tell by her reaction that the odor was strong.

Room 307 didn't look as inviting tonight. Usually, his member would be throbbing with anticipation by this point. He would picture Steven waiting in bed, willing and ready to do anything to please him.

Now, all he could think about was Ty. The whole ordeal was weighing on him heavily. He wanted to go to the police, but at this point, he knew Ty was dead. He wiped away the tear that formed in his left eye as he knocked on the door.

"Did anyone see you?" Steven asked, looking over his shoulder as he led Ricky into their room.

"No, I don't think so. I came in through the back door near the alley. I didn't see anyone around when I parked, either," Ricky said still in a daze from the events that had transpired a few hours before.

"Good. That's real good. How are you doing now?" asked Steven as he hugged Ricky. Steven began to realize that Ricky might be the reason they would get caught. He had to make sure that didn't happen.

"Not good. Not good at all." Ricky said as he pulled away from their embrace. "I can't believe that this is happening! Maybe there's still time. Maybe he isn't dead. Maybe…"

"Shut the fuck up, Ricky. God! Do you know how hard this is for me? Do you? Apparently not, because you're forgetting the fact that we both can go to jail for capital murder," Steven screamed.

"*We* didn't do this, motherfucker! *You* did this. We could have talked to Ty without hurting him, man. It could have been handled," Ricky yelled, almost knocking over the bedside lamp.

Steven pulled his arm back and slapped Ricky. The two men began to fight. They fell onto the bed, and Steven started choking Ricky.

"Now, either you're going to let this shit go, or Ty won't be the only motherfucker dead. I've already planned how to get rid of your ass, if I have to. I don't want to, but I will. You better believe that shit," Steven said in between breaths, sweating.

He waited until Ricky quit struggling and watched as Ricky coughed to regain his breath from his strong grip. Ricky's coughs turned into sobs.

In between tears, Ricky tried to explain himself. "You should have given him a chance, Steven. Ty may have been upset, but he would have listened to us. Everything would have worked out. He was a father and a husband."

"How? How would it work out? See, I don't think Ty would not have told Toni. Once he told her, it would be only a matter of time before Toni told Maya. We did what we had to do," Steven said matter of factly.

"No, *we* didn't do anything!" Ricky yelled.

"Oh, no? Who helped me? Huh? Who cleaned up? You're just as guilty as I am," Steven said with a defiant expression.

Ricky didn't respond. He just turned away. He still had no idea where Steven had put his cell. His high was gone. He only thought of Ty and Toni. These were his friends. He was their daughter's godfather. The guilt was not going to go away anytime soon. He forced himself to go to sleep. He didn't hear Steven leave.

21

MAYA

Maya's condo was still pretty far, so she decided to go to Steven's house instead. Although she didn't officially have a key, she knew where he kept the spare one.

She didn't want to go to her condo. At least she would be waking up to Steven soon. His flight was supposed to be in around six that morning.

She pulled up and grabbed her overnight bag from her backseat. She always kept one handy just in case she stayed over. The wind was blowing slightly and continued to dry her face. She could still taste the saltiness of her tears.

Maya walked around the side of Steven's house, removed the loose brick, and retrieved the spare key. The house smelled fresh. It didn't look as if he'd been there in weeks. She pressed the button to open the garage and parked inside it.

As she turned on the rest of the lights and gathered her thoughts, she noticed a credit card statement on the kitchen counter. She picked it up and began looking at the balance and charges. She had told Steven that he needed to add her to his credit card, but that conversation always seemed to go nowhere. He always made up excuse about why combining debt would not be a good idea.

When did he stay at the Hamilton? she thought. She pulled her phone out of her purse to check the dates on her calendar, ignoring Toni's missed call.

"That was the weekend he was supposed to be in Mobile, Alabama, at an at-risk youth conference," she said to herself.

Maya sat down at the kitchen table to take a look at the statement in more detail. The location definitely didn't coincide with where he said he was going, according to Google. She looked around the kitchen. She'd been there a thousand times but had never looked at it like this before. She was looking for clues.

She began going through the drawers to look for Steven's mail. All she found was utensils, ketchup packets, and junk mail. So she decided to check his office. She knew that he would spend late nights in there, preparing for upcoming cases. *Is this where he fucks this bitch when I'm not around?* she thought.

The office was filled with law books, newspaper articles, and countless awards. She pulled out his desk drawers and, sure enough, there were several bills. She looked through them until she saw a couple from Discover.

Steven went out on business trips what seemed like every few weeks. Maya specifically wanted to see if the

Hamilton Hotel appeared on the card statement. It did. On both statements, which were recent, the hotel charges coincided with out-of-town conferences. Her woman's intuition crept in slowly. *Could he be there with this bitch now?* she thought. *Maybe this is why he hasn't been answering his phone.* She pulled up the hotel on her phone and selected the call option, hoping she wouldn't find what she was looking for.

"Good evening, and thank you for calling the Hamilton Hotel. This is Greta speaking. How may I help you?" the receptionist answered as if she was amped up on Red Bull.

"Good evening, I'm looking for Mr. Steven Sims's room. Will you transfer me, please?" Maya asked, trying to sound as professional as possible.

"No, problem. Let's see: Steven, Steven Sims. Hold for your transfer, please," the receptionist said.

Maya swallowed hard. The lump in her throat was so large that it felt as if she was swallowing knives. The phone rang for what seemed like hours. Finally, a male voice answered on the other end. "Hello, hello?"

Maya hung up. It was Ricky.

22

TONI

The loud ringing from Toni's phone caused her to awake in a panic. She didn't recognize the ring or the number. She couldn't answer fast enough. The time was 3:00 a.m.

"Hello?" Toni answered. Her heart was beating so loud that she could barely hear the woman's voice on the other end.

"Hello, is this Mrs. Toni Weeks?" asked Nurse Brown.

"Yes, it is. Who is this?" Toni asked, pulling the blanket off and putting on her slippers.

"I'm Nurse Brown. I work at Sandy Springs Medical. We have your husband here," she said, bracing for the change in demeanor from Toni.

"What? Oh my God! What happened? Is he all right? Oh God!" Toni said, turning on the lights and stumbling over Jessica's toys. Her eyes were filling up with tears as the nurse began to speak.

"He's stable. He was brought in a few hours ago. He's sustained a terrible head injury. We need you here as soon as possible," the nurse stated.

"I knew something was wrong. Was he in a car accident? Oh my God," Toni cried. She was grabbing Jessica's bag, throwing on clothes, and panicking, all at the same time.

"No, ma'am. He was not in a car accident. I'm afraid it's much worse. He was found in the trunk of a car. We believe he was robbed and left for dead." Nurse Brown paused. "One more thing—we think he may be suffering from short-term memory loss. He can't remember anything after leaving work on Wednesday evening."

Nurse Brown could hear Toni crying over the phone. It saddened her tremendously to be the bearer of bad news, but it was one of the downsides of working in the emergency department.

"I can't believe this. Okay, I'm on my way. Oh God! I thought he was with Ricky. Is Ricky there? I'll be there as quick as I can," Toni said.

"Who's Ricky?" asked the nurse.

"Ricky is his best friend. He told me that he was going over his house after work," Toni explained in between sobs.

"Oh. As far as I know, he was the only one brought in, but I'll check the records to make sure. There are two detectives here. I'm sure they'll like to speak with you also," the nurse stated.

"I'll be there as soon as I can. Thanks for calling, Nurse Brown," Toni said.

With that, Toni hung up and called Carol. She didn't want Jessica to see her dad until she knew exactly what was happening. After Carol agreed to watch Jessica, Toni grabbed her daughter, who was still asleep, and headed out the door.

She tried to keep her composure, but it was hard. The night air was cool. Mrs. Carol was waiting at the door for Toni. They hugged, and Toni told her she would call her as soon as she knew what was going on with Ty.

As Toni pulled out of the garage, she Goggled the hospital. She had no idea where it was. *This is almost two hours away. Oh my God, please help me compose myself enough to make it there safely*, she thought. She took a deep breath and headed toward the interstate.

She called Ty's parents and her mom. She tried to explain what had happened as best as she could with the information provided by Nurse Brown. She also called Maya. No answer. She decided to leave a voice mail.

"Maya, something terrible has happened to Ty. I'm on my way to a hospital called Sandy Springs Medical, outside of Douglasville, Georgia. Please call me back as soon as you get this, girl. I'm scared and driving by myself. Call me," she said, trying not to sound too desperate. Even though she and Maya were at odds, Toni still needed her friend. She signaled to get into the left lane and prepared for the unknown ahead.

23

TY

The pain in Ty's head had not subsided. He'd just returned from the lab when Nurse Brown came into the room.

"Mr. Weeks, I just spoke with your wife. She's on the way," the nurse said while checking Ty's vitals.

"How is she?" Ty asked.

"She's upset, but that's to be expected. Ty, how's your pain level on a scale of one to ten?" she asked.

"My head is killing me. It's an eight, I guess," he answered.

"Okay, I'm going to get you something for that pain. Do you need anything else?" she asked.

"Not right now. I'm just trying to process all of this," Ty said while closing his eyes. The pain was definitely making him test his manhood at the moment. Toni always said he had a low tolerance for pain, and that was evident tonight. Nurse Brown left the room.

Ty was so confused. He kept replaying the last thing he remembered over and over. He had just gotten off of work and was heading home. He remembered speaking with Toni. Then he decided to call Ricky but didn't get an answer. That was all he remembered. He hoped that Toni could piece together the last twenty-four hours.

Just then Detectives Price and Reed entered the room. "Sir, we need to ask you some additional questions. It's imperative that you tell us everything," said Detective Reed.

"I'll try, but I have to tell you that I don't remember too much," said Ty.

"Just tell us what you can," said Detective Price, sounding irritated.

"After leaving work Wednesday, I got into my car to drive home. I called my wife, then I tried calling my best friend, Ricky. He did not answer. I don't remember making it home. The next thing I know, I'm waking up in the hospital," Ty said as he lay his head back on the pillow. He had become irritated. The nurse hadn't come back with the medication, and the pain was becoming unbearable.

"I see. Mr. Weeks, what type of vehicle do you drive?" asked Detective Price.

"I drive a black Chevy Impala," Ty stated.

"What year is your car?" asked Detective Reed.

"It's a 1999. It's pretty old, but it runs. Well, I guess it still runs," Ty said, disappointed. That car was the first thing he'd ever officially owned, and he treasured it for that alone.

The detectives looked at each other, confirming that the Impala was in fact the car Ty was found inside. Detective Price also noted that he needed to check Ty's recent bank and credit card transactions. The culprits may be trying to use them by now since, they couldn't find Ty's wallet.

The door opened, and Nurse Brown came in, looking concerned. She ignored the detectives. "Sorry, Mr. Weeks, I got held up filling out forms for your remaining lab work. Now, just lie back and I'll add this to your IV," she said.

Ty did as he was told. He could fill the fluid going in his veins. He closed his eyes and took a deep breath. Nurse Brown turned to the detectives. "Listen, this medication is going to knock him out for a while. Why don't you all let him get some rest? It's been a long night for him. Besides, it'll take a few days before he is completely stable," she said.

"Lady, this is a criminal investigation you're interfering with. Why the hell would you give him something to make him fall asleep in the middle of questioning?" yelled Detective Price.

"Sir, you've got a job to do, and so do I," Nurse Brown stated, visibly not giving one single fuck about what the detective had said.

The detectives left. Their only hope at this point was Ty's wife. They overheard the nurse tell Ty she was on her way.

"If his wife knows something or is involved, we'll find out," said Detective Price as he sipped his coffee.

24

RICKY

Ricky hung up the phone. He thought the hotel had rung the wrong number or something. He felt beside him, but only felt the cold of the sheets. He got up to check the bathroom. Soon, it became clear that Steven was gone, and so was Ricky's high.

His stomach began to growl. With everything that had gone on, he'd forgotten to eat. He turned on the lamp and searched for the menu for room service. Sometimes he and Steven would spend entire weekends closed up in the room, having sex and ordering room service. They hated to leave. It was their own world of erotic pleasure, filled with peace and tranquility.

Those were the weekends Ricky treasured. His wife would get on his nerves so bad during his weekends away. She would make back-to-back calls to his cell. He would simply ignore her calls. He had fallen out of love with her but decided to make himself stay with her to keep up appearances.

"Room service," said the desk clerk eagerly.

"Yes, I'd like to order the Texas cheesesteak omelet with extra mushrooms, a large side of grits, and a large sweet tea," Ricky stated.

"No problem, sir. We'll have that up to you shortly," the desk clerk replied.

Ricky went to his bag and decided to roll another joint. The weed was extra sticky, so it took a while to break down. After he rolled the joint, he went into the bathroom and turned on the shower. He decided to smoke, then shower. Within minutes, steam from the hot water filled the tiny space, along with the smoke.

He was just about dried off when he heard a knock on the door. He wrapped a towel around himself and opened the door. A cute, brown-skinned girl with curly natural hair smiled and wheeled in the tray. He gave her a twenty-dollar tip. He considered himself bisexual, and if the circumstances were different, he'd have her on his plate. The thought of fucking her in the shower made his dick hard.

As he ate, his mind raced with thoughts of Ty, Toni, and, surprisingly, Maya. He didn't know where Steven was. He hadn't left a note or anything. Ricky figured he had gone home, though. He'd known that Steven would have to leave early. *But no good-bye is fucked up*, he thought.

After nourishing his body, he searched the room for his cell. He couldn't understand what Steven wanted with it other than to stop him from telling Toni or Maya the truth. After searching for a few minutes, he found it in the nightstand. Steven had turned it off. Ricky took a deep breath and powered it on.

Within moments, the cell began updating and beeping. Ricky didn't want to face the consequences of their actions, consequences he knew would affect everyone negatively. Hi phone revealed that he has more than ten text messages and voice mails. He skipped reading the texts and pressed his voice-mail button. There it was: several frantic calls from Maya and Toni, one after another.

As he listened, Ricky's heart beat louder. Sweat beads started to form on his forehead. What seemed like a dream became a twisted and sordid reality. He wondered how long he would be able to keep up appearances while Ty was missing. His fear turned into frustration. *This is all Steven's fault*, he thought. He decided to call him.

"What's up?" Steven asked as he turned into his driveway.

"Where the fuck are you? That's what's up," Ricky yelled.

"Look, I told you I had to work today. Plus, I told Maya my flight would be due back around six," he stated nonchalantly.

Steven didn't want to disturb his neighbors with the sound of his garage, so he decided to park in the driveway. Besides, he needed the neighbors to see his car there.

"So what am I supposed to do, huh? What do I say when Toni calls me? You just get to go to work and leave me to deal with your bullshit? Is that it?" Ricky yelled.

Steven stopped himself from reacting to Ricky. He knew he needed to get inside before his neighbors heard him yelling. He quickly grabbed his bags and went inside.

"Ricky, have you lost your fucking mind? You must have forgotten who the fuck you are talking to, man. I can't baby you. You know as well as I do that we have to act as if nothing happened," he yelled.

"How the hell am I supposed to do that? How am I supposed to ignore the fact that you murdered my best friend?" Ricky cried.

"I love you, Ricky, but I am not going to risk losing Maya if we were to get found out. I told you, we did what we had to do. Now, I'm not sure how Ty found out about us, but he did. I mean, you saw how upset he was. We both agreed we did what we had to do, okay?" Steven reasoned.

"I guess you're right. I need to see you. We need to get our story straight. Remember the tux fitting today?" asked Ricky.

"Yes, I do. I'll meet you at Nikki's West for lunch around noon. I need to finish up some briefs at the office," Steven said.

"Okay. I'm going to call a cab and head home. I need to check things out and clean up again. Then I'll head that way. I love you," Ricky said calmly.

"I love you too, and remember, you never saw Ty. Don't call anyone right now or answer any calls. Say you lost your phone," said Steven. Then he hung up.

Ricky got dressed, called a cab, and walked downstairs. He felt his phone vibrate in his pocket. It was Toni calling. He pressed ignore.

25

MAYA

Forgive them father for they know not what they do.

—"Forgive Them Father," Lauryn Hill

Maya waited until she was absolutely sure Steven had left before she came out of his guest room closet. Initially, she had been prepared to confront Steven and get to the bottom of what was going on between him and Ricky. But when she heard him come in, her instinct was to hide. So she grabbed her bag, phone, and purse out of his office. Then she headed for the guestroom. She covered her mouth as she heard him talking to Ricky about Ty. Her underarms started to perspire. She prayed that he would leave. She checked her phone to make sure it was on silent.

She could not move. Her mind was in a million places. Her hiding place felt like a tomb. She didn't want to come out. So she just sat there and pondered the whole situation.

The inside of the closet was dark and smelled like stale mothballs. Maya managed to wedge herself in between a suitcase and some jackets. She prayed that Steven wouldn't go into the garage. She silently thanked God for the fact that she had parked inside it. She definitely would not have heard that conversation had Steven known she was there.

After about twenty minutes, Maya peeled herself off the floor and found the strength to turn the knob. It felt like a rebirth of some twisted sort. She had come in curious about her lover and came out knowing almost exactly who he was. It had definitely been Steven she'd heard in the background earlier that day.

She felt her heart break as she looked around the guest room. She'd thought she knew this man, but apparently he was someone else. And then there was Ricky. She knew that their relationship had been strained because of the incident with Laila, but had thought things were better since he'd introduced her to Steven. To find out that she was a part of the lie was almost too much to fathom.

What in the hell is going on? she thought. Even though she knew that Steven was gone, she tiptoed around the house, careful to not disturb anything. She tried her best not to feel defeated, but she did. Karma had won.

Maya knew that she didn't really love Steven, but she did deserve happiness. "Why does my happy ending always have to be interrupted?" she asked herself. The tears flowed as she looked around the home.

Her mind and body were weak at this point. She hadn't slept or eaten. Her mouth tasted like she'd taken a long sip of the emerald waters of the Gulf of Mexico.

She grabbed her overnight bag and tried to compose herself. *This has to be a bad dream. Maybe I didn't hear what I think I did,* she thought. She returned the key to its original spot. She backed out of Steven's garage and almost hit the mailbox.

Her nerves were shot. She replayed the conversation over and over in her head. She couldn't understand what could have happened to Ty.

The rays from the rising sun quickly shifted her perspective. She needed to get home. She needed a shower, and she needed sleep. She was sure she was delusional at this point.

Maya couldn't fathom Steven being gay. He was completely great in bed and gave head like nobody's business. There were no signs at all. And Ricky had been a ladies' man up until he'd gotten married. It just didn't make sense. She thought she'd heard it wrong.

The idea of them *doing* something to Ty turned her stomach even more. Ty and Ricky had been best friends since college. *What did Ty see?* she thought.

When Maya arrived home, she checked her phone and noticed several missed calls from Toni. She also had a few voice mails. She decided against listening to them or returning Toni's calls. She had to worry about with regaining her composure and digesting all of the insanity.

She threw down her bag and purse, headed to her medicine cabinet, and grabbed her bottle of sleeping pills. After gulping down two, she took a long shower. As she dried off, sleep was already setting in. Selfishly, she lay down in her bed and drifted off to sleep.

26

TONI

"You'll arrive at your destination in approximately ten minutes," stated the voice on Toni's Google Maps.

Toni took a deep breath and exhaled. Her jaw started to tighten as she turned into the hospital's visitor parking section. She checked her phone to see if Maya or Ricky had called, but they hadn't. She tried to not let it bother her, but the fact that she hadn't heard back from them was disconcerting. She didn't leave Ricky a voice mail, but she was certain that Maya had checked hers by now. *Some best friend,* she thought.

As Toni made her way through the huge hospital, she couldn't help but wonder what Ty had been doing out here. She knew Ricky lived near the area, but this wasn't anywhere near his house. This, coupled with the fact that Ricky hadn't returned her calls, made her wonder if something had happened to Ricky as well.

At the front desk, Toni was directed to Ty's room. She rushed down the hall, trying to hold back the tears. The tears refused to obey. She felt as if she was in line at a funeral, hearing her family members break down in front of the casket, and it was soon to be her turn.

As she approached Ty's room, Toni could see two scruffy-looking white men standing outside the door.

"Excuse me, can we help you?" asked Detective Price.

Toni told the detective that her husband was in there. She ushered herself into the room, past the detectives.

Ty was still asleep. Nurse Brown was checking his vitals when she looked up to see Toni. The two detectives came in behind her. Toni rushed to Ty's bedside.

"Ty, Ty, honey, are you okay? Oh my God! What happened to you? Ty, can you hear me?" asked Toni.

She hugged him and kissed him around his bandages. He didn't look like the same man she'd come to know and love all these years. For the first time, he looked helpless. The possibility of losing Ty became overwhelming, and Toni broke down.

The detectives stood in the doorway, carefully observing Toni. As far as they were concerned, everyone was a suspect.

Nurse Brown walked over to Toni and gently patted her on the back. "Hi, I'm Nurse Brown. I was the one who called you earlier," she said. "Please sit down. He's stable and needs to rest now. He's in a lot of pain, I'm sad to say."

"Toni, Toni Weeks," Toni replied in between sobs. "I'm sorry. I just can't believe this is happening."

"I know it's a lot to take in, but you have to be strong for him. If he wakes up and sees you upset like this, it's only going to make him upset."

"You're right. You're absolutely right. I'm just in shock. Please tell me what happened to my husband."

Nurse Brown handed Toni some Kleenex and began. "Well, Mr. Weeks was brought in late last night. He was found in the trunk of a car. He'd suffered a major blow to the head and lost a lot of blood. He has been talking, but he doesn't remember what happened to him. We believe he may be suffering from short-term memory loss."

Toni put her head in her hands. "What about Ricky? He was supposed to go see his best friend, Ricky. Is Ricky here?" Toni asked, looking back up.

Just then, the detectives walked over. "Excuse me, I'm Detective Reed and this is Detective Price. We've been assigned to this case. Do you mind if we ask you a few questions?" Detective Reed asked.

Toni reluctantly agreed and asked the nurse to come get her as soon as Ty woke up. She stepped out into the hallway with the detectives, fearful of what to expect. She couldn't understand what was happening.

"As the nurse stated, your husband was found in the trunk of a car at a parking lot not very far from here. Some pedestrians heard him yelling from inside and called the police. He wasn't found with anything on him. No wallet or wedding ring was recovered. Looks like he was robbed and left for dead. Mrs. Weeks, where were you tonight?" asked Detective Reed.

"I was home, waiting for Ty to come back from Ricky's house," Toni replied.

"I see. Can someone verify your whereabouts?"

"Yes, my best friend Maya and my neighbor Carol. Carol kept my daughter for a few hours while I went with Maya yesterday evening."

"And where did you and Maya go?" asked Detective Price, getting a bit antsy.

"Well, Maya called me and said that she was concerned about her fiancé, so I rode with her to find him."

"And did you find him?"

"No, he actually called her before we found him, so we turned around and she brought me back home."

"We heard you mention Ricky to the nurse back there. You mind telling us who that person is?" asked Detective Price.

"He's my husband's best friend. His name is Ricky Davis." Toni exhaled. "Ty hadn't heard from Ricky in a few days and told me he was going to go visit him yesterday."

"Where does Ricky live?" asked Detective Reed.

"He lives in Douglasville, about thirty minutes or so from here, I would suspect. I've been trying to reach him also," said Toni.

"When was the last time you saw your husband?"

"Yesterday morning before he left for work."

"Did you all argue or have any problems in your marriage?"

"No, we didn't argue, and everybody has problems in their marriage. We're not perfect, by no means, but I love him and he loves me."

"Okay, we'll, uh, let you get back to your husband. We'll be in touch. Thanks," said Detective Price.

Toni nodded and returned to Ty's room.

The two detectives compared notes. It seemed quite odd to them that Toni was so forthcoming with the fact that she had not been at home yesterday evening.

"Either she is telling us the truth or she's a dumb bitch for not sticking to the fact that she was *only* at home. Let's go see Ricky Davis," said Detective Price as he held the elevator door for his partner.

27

TY

Ty woke up with a slight jolt. While he was asleep, he had dreamed of being in a dark place. He could tell that he was wrapped up in something. All he could think about was getting out and surviving. The dream disturbed him a lot because it seemed so real.

He looked to his left, and there was Toni. She was asleep in the recliner next to his bed. He didn't want to wake her. She looked so peaceful. The last thing he wanted to do was disturb her rest. Instead, he just watched her and reveled in her beauty. He was relieved that she was there. The place didn't feel as lonely anymore.

Nurse Brown came in, and Ty motioned for her to be quiet. She eased over to him, being careful not to wake Toni. She checked his vitals and temperature.

"How is your pain level?" she asked.

"It's all right. I don't feel the pounding like I did before. I just feel a lot of pressure."

"Well, that's to be expected. You do have some slight swelling, but it should subside in the next few days."

"How soon will I be able to go home?" he asked.

"Hmm, once your tests come back, it'll be a few days. This is assuming that your swelling has gone down and depending on how you're healing."

"What about my memory? Will I remember what happened to me?"

"That's hard to say, Ty. Most people in your situation only regain partial memories, but I'm not going to say it's impossible."

Ty fought back the tears that were forming in his eyes. He wanted the person or persons who had done this to him to be caught. He wanted to tell them that they didn't win. He wanted them to know that he didn't die.

"Wow. I keep replaying leaving work in my mind. It's as clear as day," said Ty. "How I went from driving home to the trunk of my car, bleeding, is mind blowing. I mean, I'm a good guy, Nurse Brown. I work, and I take care of my responsibilities as a man. Don't get me wrong, now, I'm not perfect. But I try my best to do right. I'm a father and a husband. I didn't deserve this."

Ty began to get angrier and angrier as he thought about his situation. *Those motherfuckers are going to pay for this,* he thought.

"Ty, I'm in here almost every day, and believe me when I tell you that bad things happen to good people. You just better be glad that you are laid up in this hospital bed and not the morgue," Nurse Brown said matter of factly. "Get some rest. I'll be back to check on you soon. Betty will bring y'all some breakfast in a few."

She had to leave. She hated to get so personal with Ty, but he needed a reality check. Most people in his situation would just be glad to be alive and in their right mind. *He should be counting his lucky stars,* she thought as she walked to her next patient.

Toni woke up when she heard the door close. Her eyes met Ty's stare. Ty's face was swollen. His lips looked blue. His left eye was slightly closed due to the bandages. She silently prayed for strength. She was adamant about being strong for her husband.

"Hi, baby. How are you feeling?" she asked as walked over to his bedside.

"Better now that you're here."

"What in the world, Ty? I was so scared. I'm just glad that you are alive. Thank God! I am so sorry this happened to you, baby. Can I get you anything?

"You can get me my memory back. Toni, I don't remember anything since I left work on Wednesday. I can't even begin to tell you how that feels. Talk to me, baby. Tell me something. Maybe it will jog my memory."

Toni took a deep breath. "Well, you called me and said you'd be home in a few minutes. You got home, ate and..."

"What did I eat?" Ty interrupted.

"You ate fried catfish and homemade hush puppies. You read a book to Jessica, um, took a shower, and tried calling Ricky. You complained that he hasn't been returning your calls or texts. You said that you were going to go to his house and check on him after you got off work Thursday."

"Anything else?"

Toni blushed. "We made love, and we went to sleep."

"Hold up, we made love? I hate that I don't remember that. Was it good?"

"Yes baby, it was. It always is good," she laughed.

"Yes, it is. You better be glad I'm all battered and bruised, girl, because your sweet pussy sounds like a very good idea right about now. But anyway, did I go to work Thursday?

"Yeah, you were supposed to get off early, though. You were going to go see Ricky," she said.

"Damn, speaking of Ricky, have you spoken to him yet? I mean, did I ever go see him?" Ty asked with a frowned expression.

"Baby, I've tried calling Ricky over and over. I called you both all night, and so did Maya. I have not heard from him. That's why I asked the nurse if Ricky was here. Hell, I was worried that something happened to him too." she answered clearly as confused as Ty was about his best friend's absence.

"I have to talk to Ricky. It doesn't make sense. This is getting strange as hell." said Ty.

"You're right, it doesn't make sense. I haven't heard from Maya, either. Do you know she had me riding with her last night, thinking Steven was cheating on her? But that's a story for another time."

"Wow. So where is Jessica?" Ty asked. The last thing he wanted to do right now was hear about Maya and her antics.

"She's with Mrs. Carol. I'm about to call and check on her. I called your parents. They are on the way from Gordo." Toni stated.

"I wish you hadn't called them. You know how much my mom worries."

"I know, but she'd kill me if I didn't tell her, and you know it. She barely likes me as it is." Toni reasoned.

Just then, the door opened, interrupting their conversation. In walked an older white lady wearing green scrubs.

"Good morning," she said. "I'm Betty, and I brought y'all some breakfast. Mr. Weeks, you can only have broth right now. We want to see if you can hold down liquids. Mrs. Weeks, I brought you some coffee, bagels, and fruit."

"Thanks, Betty," Toni said as she grabbed the tray and placed it on the counter. "I'll make sure he eats it."

"Okay, let me help him up," said Betty. After she had adjusted Ty's bed, she left the couple.

"Now, let me feed you baby," Toni said as she gently blew on the broth to cool it.

"Ugh! This shit is disgusting," said Ty after he'd had a spoonful.

"Well, you have to try to eat. You've been through a lot. Just think of it as getting your strength back."

Once Ty was finished eating, like clockwork, Nurse Brown came back into the room. This time she had the doctor with her. They went over Ty's test results and told them that he'd have to be kept a few more days for observation. His stitches were checked for any bleeding.

"I'm going to step out and make a few calls, Ty. Do you need anything?" Toni asked.

Ty shook his head. What he needed were answers. The pain had come back again. He motioned for Nurse Brown to give him more medicine, and his thoughts turned to Ricky.

28

RICKY

The house didn't look the same to Ricky when he entered. It felt cold and uninviting. He stood in the doorway of his bedroom and gazed around. So much had taken place in that particular room. He'd made passionate love to his ex-wife Laila there. He'd fucked Steven there, and now his best friend had been murdered there.

The realization made tears fall without him even noticing. He took a deep breath and snapped out of it. He began to look at the room as a crime scene and starting recleaning. He made a mental note to put the house on the market after all the shit blew over.

The bleach was so strong that he had to open the windows. He scrubbed down the walls and made sure he had the lamp wrapped up in the trash. He was shocked at how easy it was to wipe away the evidence. He started to feel better after he showered.

He wanted to see Steven. This would just be another secret they'd share. The thought of his lover made his member rise. He wanted to fuck Steven. He needed to release himself inside of Steven. He licked his lips in anticipation. He'd seen the new house in Pemberbrook and couldn't wait to fuck Steven in every room. Sure, he'd be married to Maya, but Ricky knew she couldn't satisfy Steven the way he could. Before he knew it, he was jacking off in the shower. The hot water and the feeling of his hands stroking his dick made him cum quickly. Loud knocking on the door interrupted his self-pleasuring session. *Who the hell can that be?* he thought.

He grabbed his robe, looked the window, and saw a black Crown Vic in his driveway. He looked out the peephole and saw two white guys. *What the fuck?* he thought.

"Just a second!" he yelled as he threw on sweatpants and a T-shirt. He exhaled and opened the door.

"Mr. Davis, I presume?" asked Detective Reed. Ricky nodded. "I'm Detective Reed, and this is my partner Detective Price. Do you mind if we ask you a few questions?"

"No, not at all," Ricky said as he stepped outside.

"Pretty strong bleach smell, isn't it?" asked Detective Price.

"What can I help you with, gentlemen?" Ricky asked, ignoring the detective's question.

"Do you know Ty Weeks?" asked Detective Reed.

"Of course, that's my best friend. Why, is he okay?"

"Mr. Davis, where were you last night?" asked Detective Price, ignoring Ricky's question like Ricky had ignored his.

"I was at home."

"Did Ty Weeks come visit you yesterday?" asked Detective Price.

"No, he texted me earlier, but I never saw him. I texted him back, but he never responded. We are supposed to be meeting up today in Birmingham for a tuxedo fitting later. Is something wrong?"

Ricky was visibly shaken. Sweat beads started to form on his forehead. His armpits were perspiring. His heart started to race. He was afraid of what the detectives were going to say next.

"Mr. Weeks was found last night not too far from your home. He was badly hurt and was in the trunk of his car."

"Oh my God! I can't believe this. Is he dead?" asked Ricky. He would have collapsed on his porch if it were not for Detective Reed catching him. He started sobbing uncontrollably. He could have received an Oscar for that performance.

"Calm down, Mr. Davis. He's okay. He was taken to the hospital and is in stable condition," said Detective Reed.

Ricky's waterworks changed quickly to confusion. He raised his head, looking puzzled. Both detectives noticed.

"He's okay? That is great news. I have to go see him." Ricky tried to walk back into the house as if he were leaving that very second.

"Not so fast, Mr. Davis. Mr. Weeks is having a tough time remembering what happened to him. Do you know anybody who would want to hurt him?" asked Detective Price, watching Ricky's every move.

"No, I don't."

"Any problems at home with his missus? Problems with coworkers?"

"Well, all marriages have problems. Toni doesn't work, so how miserable can she be?" Ricky said jokingly.

The detectives noted his strange behavior. He seemed to be anxious all of a sudden. They gave each other the *he may be involved* look.

"Is there anything else, gentlemen? I'd like to get dressed and check on my friend, if I can. What is the name of the hospital?" asked Ricky.

"We'll be in touch," said Detective Price. Without giving Ricky an answer, the detectives got in their Crown Vic and left.

Ricky ran inside and called Steven. His heart was racing so fast that he was sure it would stop at any minute. Steven didn't answer his phone. Ricky decided that it would be a bad idea to leave a message. He paced back and forth. He wanted to call Toni, but he felt he needed to talk to Steven first. Plus, Toni would expect him to come to the hospital. He wasn't sure if he could face Ty yet. All he could think about was *What did Ty remember?* His body felt limp. He gathered his thoughts, got dressed, and headed to Birmingham.

29

MAYA

My God is my judge; no gown, no gavel.

—"Misunderstood," Lil Wayne

The sound of thunder awakened Maya. She rolled over to check the clock on her nightstand. It was three o'clock in the afternoon. She yawned as she noticed the red light on her phone. Her stomach growled. She stretched and grabbed her phone.

There was a voice mail from Toni. Her heart fell. She knew what it was about. She didn't want to face it yet. She crawled out of bed and went to her bathroom. The double vanity, large whirlpool tub, and separate shower looked different on that cloudy day. Usually the light would make the fixtures sparkle.

Maya ran a bubble bath and brushed her teeth. As hard as she tried, she couldn't help but look at her reflection.

Her face didn't look the same. The sleeping pills made her groggy. The temporary escape hadn't lasted as long as she had hoped.

Disappointed, she grabbed her phone and sat in the tub. She thought back to the overheard conversation at Steven's house and to the sound of Steven yelling at Ricky before that. There were so many unanswered questions. She couldn't fathom the idea of Steven and Ricky being gay. *There has to be another explanation,* she thought. *Maybe Ricky is using Steven's card. That's probably the reason he answered. But where does Ty fit in to all of this? And what happened to Ty?*

The only way to get to the bottom of this was her phone. She closed her eyes after pressing dial. And there it was. There was Toni's voice on the other end, telling her about Ty. *Damn,* she thought. She hung up her phone and saw a text from Steven. It said that his flight had just gotten in and he'd had to postpone the tuxedo fitting until next week. It also said that he loved her and couldn't wait to see her later tonight.

Maya lay back in the tub to ponder her dilemma: whether or not she wanted to risk it all for the sake of everyone else or choose to remain silent and continue as if she never knew a thing. She also hoped that with everything going on, Toni would forget what she'd said about overhearing Steven yell at Ricky. As she thought back over the past few years, she chose to stay quiet.

She frowned. *Toni deserves exactly what she gets,* she thought. *If she hadn't fucked Ty, she wouldn't be going through all of this. Why should I risk my happiness for her? I'm so close to having the dream life I've always wanted. The dream life I deserve. The dream life that was stolen from me. Fuck that! No one knows what I heard. I have the right to remain silent. I've invested time in my relationship. We've already purchased a home. The announcement has already been placed in the paper. I'm almost there. I'm almost Mrs. Sims, and I'm not going to ruin that for anybody, not even my best friend.*

With her mind made up, Maya finished her bath and called Steven. "Hey, baby! How are you?" she asked.

"I'm doing much better now that I can hear your voice. I called you earlier. Did you get my text?"Steven asked.

"I did. It's fine. You have plenty of time to get fitted for your tux. How was your trip?"Maya asked.

"Good. I was extremely busy. You know how it is. I haven't been able to stop thinking about you, though. How about dinner tonight?"

"Dinner tonight sounds good, as long as I'm on the menu," she laughed.

"Oh, I plan to make you my dessert. You know I've been wanting to kiss both lips. Let's go to Texas De Brazil."

"Sounds like a plan to me. Text me the details, baby. Bye now." Maya smiled as she hung up.

Maya planned on calling Toni, but she definitely wasn't going to the hospital. Not that day, anyway. She wanted to enjoy being the blushing bride and the thoughtful friend who had misplaced her phone—or at least appear to, anyway.

She lay naked on her bed and thought of the lovemaking session she'd have later on that night. She licked her fingers and gently glided them into the moistness between her thighs. She was wet even after drying off. The more she felt her juices, the more excited she became. She laughed to herself, knowing that while she would be getting her brains fucked out, Toni would be sitting in a hospital, miserable. *Karma is a bitch,* she thought as she climaxed all over her white silk sheets.

30

TONI

Ty reached up to feel the stitches in his head through the bandages. Toni knew that this whole ordeal would be a huge blow to his ego. He's always been the one to take care of her. She watched the pained look in her husband's eyes and couldn't help but feel pain as well. The difficult task of trying to maintain her own sanity while dealing with his weighed on her heavily.

She checked her phone. There was still no word from Maya or Ricky. She shook her head. It was almost five o'clock. She knew damn well that they had seen her calls. The thought pissed her off.

"How are you feeling now, baby?" she asked.

"I'm okay. My stomach is still queasy, though," Ty replied.

"It's probably the medication that caused you to throw up, like the nurse said. You'll be all right."

"Will I? I mean, here I am in this hospital bed, and the motherfuckers that did this are somewhere chilling!"

"Calm down, Ty. I know you're upset. Hell, I am upset too, but that shouldn't be our focus. Our focus should be on you getting better. Just try to take it easy, please," Toni said.

"Toni, I can't take it easy when I can't even remember what happened to me. I can't tell you what it feels like," Ty replied.

"Well, the doctor said that it is possible for you to remember. It'll come; just be patient, baby. I'm as angry as you are, but I'm grateful that I'm not planning your funeral."

"I don't want to seem ungrateful, but this bothers me."

Toni got up and hugged Ty. She knew that what he needed now was support. That was all she had to give at this point.

"How you heard anything from Ricky?" asked Ty.

Toni exhaled. "Nope. I've called him over and over. I don't know what's going on with him. I haven't heard from Maya either."

"Now there's a shocker," he said sarcastically.

"Don't start that shit, Ty."

"Don't start what? Toni, Maya is not your friend. I don't know why you refuse to accept that. She's never there for you, but you are always there for her."

"She's there for me," Maya said, hoping that Ty wouldn't ask for examples.

"How? You said it yourself that every single time you need her, she always has an excuse. I'm tired of you wasting your time with her, Toni."

"First of all, I'm not wasting my time. Secondly, Maya is not that bad. We've known each other for years. For the most part, she means well."

"'For the most part, she means well'? Do you hear yourself? Did she mean well when she didn't see Jessica until she was six weeks old? She didn't even bother to show up for your baby shower, and you turn around and make her a godmother. And don't even get me started on the little digs she constantly takes at you." Ty reminded her.

"What do you expect, Ty? I deserve it after what I did to her." Toni stated bluntly.

"Oh, come on! That was years ago. We've all moved on. She should have moved on by now. You can't keep apologizing for the past. It's not going to change anything. What's done is done, Toni." Ty said.

"I'm not living in the past. I just try to put myself in her shoes. I mean, I don't know what I would do if the situation was reversed."

"If she couldn't handle it, she should have said 'fuck it' a long time ago. I'm tired of the back-and-forth shit between you two. And I'm tired of the way she treats you. She knows that you have a good heart. She's taking advantage of your guilt. Can't you see that?" Ty asked visibly upset.

"Is it that you don't want her around because she bothers me? Or is it because she bothers you?"Toni asked snapping her neck like Shananay from the sitcom Martin.

"And what is that supposed to mean?"Ty asked.

"Oh, you know *exactly* what it means. You don't think I see the way she looks at you? I'm not stupid, Ty. Are you afraid you feel the same way she does?

"Oh, come on now. Listen to yourself, Toni. You know damn well I don't want Maya. But you know she still wants me, huh? Why be friends with someone like that?"

"Because I'm your second choice, Ty. That's why."

"Look Toni, I—"

Toni interrupted him. "I'll be back. I'm going to the Starbucks downstairs."

She had to leave before the conversation got more heated. She knew that Maya was no good, but she hated the fact that Ty had pointed it out. The last thing she wanted to do today was defend Maya or their friendship.

It took the elevator forever to get there. Toni found herself holding back her tears as she pressed the button for floor two. The hospital was packed. She knew she looked rough and prayed that the caffeine would add life to her weary body.

The line at Starbucks was long. She decided to wait anyway. She needed to cool down. She shifted from one foot to the other until it was her turn in line. She didn't notice Laila sitting at the table a few feet from her.

Laila was reading the paper as she waited for her white-chocolate mocha. She was at the hospital waiting for her sister to deliver her third child. She was surprised to turn the page to the wedding section and see that her ex-husband's lover was marrying Maya. She was so shocked at the picture that she dropped the paper by accident. As she bent down to pick it up, she saw Toni.

mwisho

An excerpt from Appearances Too

Detectives Price and Reed arrived back at the hospital. They'd reviewed the parking lot cameras but the security lights were blown so the image was shaky at best. All they could make out was the vehicle pulling in and some tall figure getting out. The camera faced the back of the person's head so there was nothing concrete.

Detective Reed made notations of Ricky's physical appearance. He felt like Ricky had something to do with it. It was all a matter of proving it as far as he was concerned. What he couldn't figure out was a motive. He'd checked Ricky's background and didn't see anything that would show ill intent towards his best friend. *It has to be something we are overlooking*, he thought...

Made in the USA
San Bernardino, CA
10 June 2017